Writ in Water

Writ in Water

A novel of John Keats

by James Sulzer

FUZE
PUBLISHING

Ashland, Oregon

Book design by Ray Rhamey

ISBN 978-1-7330344-2-5

Library of Congress Control Number: 2021905364

For Barbara

Bright star, steadfast

Contents

Ode to a Nightingale

My heart aches, and a drowsy numbness pains
    My sense, as though of hemlock I had drunk,
Or emptied some dull opiate to the drains
    One minute past, and Lethe-wards had sunk:
'T is not through envy of thy happy lot,
    But being too happy in thine happiness,—
        That thou, light-winged Dryad of the trees,
            In some melodious plot
Of beechen green, and shadows numberless,
        Singest of summer in full-throated ease.

O, for a draught of vintage! that hath been
    Cool'd a long age in the deep-delved earth,
Tasting of Flora and the country-green,
    Dance, and Provençal song, and sunburnt mirth!
O for a beaker full of the warm South,
    Full of the true, the blushful Hippocrene,
        With beaded bubbles winking at the brim,
            And purple-stained mouth;
That I might drink, and leave the world unseen,
        And with thee fade away into the forest dim:

Fade far away, dissolve, and quite forget
    What thou among the leaves hast never known,
The weariness, the fever, and the fret
    Here, where men sit and hear each other groan;
Where palsy shakes a few, sad, last grey hairs,
    Where youth grows pale, and spectre-thin, and dies;
        Where but to think is to be full of sorrow
            And leaden-eyed despairs;
    Where Beauty cannot keep her lustrous eyes,
        Or new Love pine at them beyond to-morrow.

Away! away! for I will fly to thee,
    Not charioted by Bacchus and his pards,
But on the viewless wings of Poesy,
    Though the dull brain perplexes and retards:
Already with thee! tender is the night,
    And haply the Queen-Moon is on her throne,
        Cluster'd around by all her starry Fays;
            But here there is no light,
    Save what from heaven is with the breezes blown
        Through verdurous glooms and winding mossy ways.

I cannot see what flowers are at my feet,
    Nor what soft incense hangs upon the boughs,
But, in embalmed darkness, guess each sweet
    Wherewith the seasonable month endows
The grass, the thicket, and the fruit-tree wild;
    White hawthorn, and the pastoral eglantine;
        Fast fading violets cover'd up in leaves;
            And mid-May's eldest child,
    The coming musk-rose, full of dewy wine,
        The murmurous haunt of flies on summer eves.

Darkling I listen; and, for many a time
    I have been half in love with easeful Death,
Call'd him soft names in many a mused rhyme,
    To take into the air my quiet breath;
Now more than ever seems it rich to die,
    To cease upon the midnight with no pain,
        While thou art pouring forth thy soul abroad
            In such an ecstasy!
    Still wouldst thou sing, and I have ears in vain—
        To thy high requiem become a sod.

Thou wast not born for death, immortal Bird!
    No hungry generations tread thee down;
The voice I hear this passing night was heard
    In ancient days by emperor and clown:
Perhaps the self-same song that found a path
      Through the sad heart of Ruth, when, sick for home,
          She stood in tears amid the alien corn;
             The same that oft-times hath
Charm'd magic casements, opening on the foam
      Of perilous seas, in faery lands forlorn.

Forlorn! the very word is like a bell
    To toll me back from thee to my sole self!
Adieu! the fancy cannot cheat so well
    As she is fam'd to do, deceiving elf.
Adieu! adieu! thy plaintive anthem fades
    Past the near meadows, over the still stream,
          Up the hill-side; and now 't is buried deep
             In the next valley-glades:
Was it a vision, or a waking dream?
          Fled is that music:—do I wake or sleep?

I

N

It was a curious sight.

Three of the wingless creatures known as humans stood in a row. Each of them straddled a skinny two-wheeled thing with one large wheel in front and a smaller one behind. Planting their feet under them, the men shoved themselves forward with great thrusts of their legs. The wheels hummed like honeybees.

Directly in their path sat a young man, his head cradled in his arms. I wondered if he was in pain. He looked up as the travelers zipped up to him and stopped just short of his face. They called out to him in the harshest of voices:

Cockney poet!

Never was there a young man so encrusted with conceit!

Back to the apothecary shop, Mr. John, back to plasters, pills, and ointment boxes!

Then, perfectly in time, they each lifted a leg like a dog and released a spray of liquid that splashed onto the face and chest of the young man. The deed done, they galloped off on their wheeled mounts.

Adding to the strangeness, all this was happening in midair, in the deepening dusk, in the middle of a great city, high above a broad flight of worn grey stairs and a vast nest of stone buildings and fountains.

❧⋆⋆

A young woman, clothed in the color of leaves, flickered up to the dripping young man and perched near him. Her face was long and smooth, and her mouth was the red of berries.

As I've said before, I wish to be appreciated for more than mere beauty. I have never loved nor never will love you, John.

She turned and walked off on the arm of a tall man in a red jacket and a high black cap.

⁕〜(ʊʊ)〜⁕

A dried-up old man in breeches and half boots glided into sight, seated at a great desk and patting a bag that overflowed with a shiny metal. He pointed his nose, sharp and protruding like the beak of a raven, toward the young man.

You again? It was almost more than I could bear, trying to usher the wayward Keats brood into lives as responsible adults. After your parents left you with nothing but their weakness for sins of the flesh and of the bottle.

I am not here to listen to your insults, the young man replied.

Then I suppose you have come again to ask for money. But it's a bit too late for that now, don't you think? Do I need to remind you of your boast, "I mean to rely upon my abilities as a poet"?

He extended a long arm, plunged a claw into the young man's chest, and tore out his heart. He dropped it to the floor, where it fluttered like the wings of a wounded sparrow.

With a dry chuckle, Raven man turned his attention back to the columns of figures on the parchment before him.

⁕〜(ʊʊ)〜⁕

Somewhere inside me, in the place where songs are born, I knew I needed to stay with this young man and keep him company.

But why? What could I offer him?

We are simple birds.

We sing. We eat. We sleep.

We sing of summer in full-throated ease and are no strangers to ecstasy. When it is time, we depart from this earth with no care or concern for what comes next.

True, I had met him once or twice before. For several hours early one morning, I trilled my songs high in the boughs of my plum tree while he—quite alive then—lounged in a chair below, glancing up every now and then. I could tell he was listening closely, and I added some special, joyful notes. It wasn't long before his hand sprang to life and began to fill up some white squares with long trails of those things they call *words*.

There might have been one brief, earlier encounter as well.

But that was all.

When I am near him now, I feel a strange tug—as if I owe him something. Something feels incomplete, like at the start of nest-building season, but what could it be?

The young man was hunched over again. I darted up to him, intending to demand, What do I owe you?

But no song sprang forth. Several times I tried—nothing. Not a whistle, trill, warble, buzz. I was silent.

Yet somehow he realized I was there, for he glanced up at me. I will never forget the look in his eyes.

He was in pain. More than pain. The young man was in peril.

J

Nothing ever becomes real till it is experienced. All my life and death remain a mystery but for one certainty.

In every dream that I cherished, I failed.

No epic poem to number me among the English poets. No great love that bottled up its fiery beginnings, then mellowed over a lifetime like a fine vintage. No wise insights that could offer light and hope to the lives of men and women.

My one success was an intimate acquaintance with pain— physical and mental anguish. In all else, I fell short.

In truth, I have only myself to blame. I vowed early on that I would sooner fail than not be among the greatest.

The last few months of my life, as I languished in a fevered dream in Rome, felt like a posthumous existence. But what was then a simile has become my new reality. Where is the mood, the tense, the syntax to capture this?

Wafting above the Spanish Steps like a hot-air balloon, I have stalled over an open area. Could this be some sort of way station? Beneath me my life unravels, scattered like a pack of cards.

What bashful and curious spirit is this that gleams in the dusk beside me? As small as a tumbler, as wayward as a firefly, it flits here and there but never quite leaves my side.

Do you know who I am? Or was? Or hoped to be? I ask.

It flutters before me as if listening.

I was a poet.

N

A poet. A maker of verse. A singer of songs.

By now the poet and I had risen about as high above the broad stone steps as the canopy of my plum tree.

The poet was hunched over again, his head inclined upon his arm.

From out of the gloom, a squarish shape drifted into sight and revealed itself to be a bed with a pale young man stretched upon it. His head was turned to the side, and a line of spit dribbled down his jaw. Slowly and with effort, he wiped it off on his blanket. He forced himself to sit up and shape his lips into a smile.

I am better now. You must go on your hike to the north, John. You must learn how to be a poet.

At the sound of his voice, the poet looked up. His eyes grew round, and he opened his mouth as if to speak. He jumped to his feet.

A swarm of insects descended on the pale young man's face, covering it with their scarlet bodies and wriggling black legs, and commenced to feast on the boy's flesh. They flew off, leaving behind a naked skull with chattering teeth.

The poet called, *No, Tom! No!*

The bed floated off into the dusk.

※ ᭰᭣ᨪ᭱ ᪥

The poet collapsed like the flimsy nest of a dove.

A man with a puffed-up chest like a pigeon stood before him, his thumbs tucked into his vest. He paced back and forth as if searching for food.

You have led me on step by step, day by day. It is no secret that I require your financial aid in order to complete my great work of art, Christ's Entry *into Jerusalem. Which features you prominently, as you know, next to Wordsworth and Newton. Can there be any other explanation for your behavior than monstrous ingratitude?*

※〜(つつ)〜※

Pigeon man shrank into the distance to the size of a robin's egg, then popped out of sight. A young girl now appeared before us, striding back and forth in a cramped room and stopping now and then to glance out the tiny window.

John, why don't you answer my summons? I am in crisis in my relations with Mr. and Mrs. Abbey. Why won't you contact me?

Before the poet could reply, the young girl opened her mouth so wide that darkness rushed in and obliterated her.

Yes, obliterated her. And obliterated the poet's hope for making a reply.

Obliterate. It's one of the thousands and thousands of words that I have recently struggled to learn. Along with *peril* and *flimsy* and *straddle* and countless others.

This form of communication was granted to me at my passing, and I'm doing my best to understand how it works.

So many words, and all so different.

Summer.

A fat, round word like a juicy beetle, full of warmth and goodness.

Fever.

A skinny and troubled word, as worrisome as a hawk circling overhead.

I've found that words don't usually exist alone, but in combination with others. In the voice of the poet, I hear them issue in endless variety.

The weariness, the fever, and the fret.

The exact meaning is outside my understanding, but I know enough to realize that the taste is bitter.

Though these phrases confuse me, I value the skill that creates them. Nightingales possess a similar skill. We pride ourselves on our ability to weave precise arrangements of sounds and song fragments into an intricate and beautiful pattern. A pattern that we can repeat to perfection.

Because each word that humans use already contains its own separate nest of meaning, any combination of words creates a larger nest where the meanings connect to others in ways that are difficult to follow.

But I've begun to understand enough to make some guesses about the lives of the earthbound. I sense cold winds and storms at the heart of their beings. The poet is no stranger to suffering, and as he seems to review his life, he is coming upon much that is painful.

What, I wonder, can be the point of humans' struggles and despair? *Where but to think is to be full of sorrow.*

Sorrow ... another word, for something that I met rarely in my life. The egg in my nest was Joy.

But now, after a life of song and ease, I feel a strange incompleteness, which flares when I am near the poet. Why?

I can hear him voicing his thoughts again. It seems he cannot hear mine—so I am able to take the private measure of his being. Already it is clear that he has left some things unfinished.

I wonder. Out of those many broken strands, could I help him weave a final nest?

J

Long ago, when we were children, didn't I try to make things right for my siblings and myself—to balance the ledger? Make a great success. Achieve immortality and thereby save us from the early loss of our parents, when they left us alone in this vale of tears.

I intended to triumph and had little doubt that I would. But life throws up any number of obstacles. First and worst was the stingy guardian of our family estate, who blocked my every turn.

As I suffer my painful review of the fragments of memory that inhabit this halfway world, the vexing spirit hovers beside me, observing me in silence. Its flutters there and about seem to betray a tremulous uncertainty. I suspect that something is threatened or amiss in its world, as it is in mine, but what that may be is impossible to know.

I sense a kind disposition but also a paucity of understanding. It is a different quality of being than I, lighter and freer. The way it flits about like a dragonfly, it reminds me of a light-winged dryad of my past.

How fortunate an existence it must be, merely to live, with no obligation to choose one's path through the perils of the world.

III

N

The poet and I floated higher into the atmosphere, far enough above the earth to observe the blue-black curve of the horizon.

A small, spare room drifted into view, revealing a girl seated on the bed.

John, the Abbeys are so cruel to me! You must help me!

There were many times—too many to count—when I should have helped her, the poet announced to the darkness.

They are cruel to you, too. They say you have thrown your life away. They say you will never amount to anything.

Yes, they would say that.

And when I speak up on your behalf, they lock me in this room without supper. Please, John, I beg you, won't you come visit me?

The girl faded into the dusk, and the poet bowed his head.

※〜(ご)〆※

What happened next was somehow my doing yet at the same time outside my powers. Was it I who made the ground beneath us ripple and shimmer like a pool of water when a heron touches down? If not I, who?

J

What appears below us is astonishing. It is the morning after the death of our grandmother Alice in December 1814. At the age of nineteen I am now an orphan—along with my younger brothers George and Tom and my little sister Fanny—with no one to look after us but the trustee of our grandfather's estate, Mr. Richard Abbey.

Mr. Abbey's countinghouse is a large brick building near the river. When I push open the solid oaken door, George, Tom, and Fanny are already huddled together by the fire in the front room. Fanny lets out a cry and runs to me, burying her face against my shoulder.

"Oh, John!" she cries. "What will become of us now?" She is skinny as a sapling and taller than I remember from my visit a few months earlier. But she is as sensitive and impulsive as ever.

"There, there, Fanny," I try to soothe her. "We still have each other."

She wipes the tears from her eyes and gazes up at me. Her long, narrow face looks older than her eleven years. Her hazel eyes are quick and observant.

"John, it's horrid," she murmurs. "I will be forced to live with the Abbeys." She lets out a shriek, shakes her head, and buries it again on my shoulder.

"Shh," I caution her. "Mr. Abbey holds great power over us. But I do believe we can trust him to be fair."

I observe the swell of her cheek on my shoulder and remember when she was three years old, how she would climb into my lap at supper, ask to eat off my plate, and stuff food into her mouth. She knew I couldn't refuse her. "You're my favorite brother," she liked to whisper into my ear with her breathy little food-spattered voice.

Our youngest brother Tom, pale and thin, and middle brother George, the largest and strongest by far of us all, are

standing aside awkwardly. Tom starts to weep and presses his fingers to his forehead; George sighs and droops his
head.

Fanny hugs me closer. "Can you recite something for us?"
she asks in a tiny voice.

I step back, gather myself, and begin.

> As from the darkening gloom a silver dove
> Upsoars, and darts into the Eastern light,
> On pinions that naught moves but pure delight;
> So fled thy soul into the realms above.

I pause. Fanny has been watching me closely. "John, that's
lovely. What is it?"

"Oh, it's a poem I'm working on."

"Is it about Grandmother?"

I nod, and she claps her hands. "You should be a poet, not
a surgeon."

Ten hollow footsteps sound above us, slow and deliberate.
Fanny throws me a worried look.

Richard Abbey has descended the wooden stairs from his
office and lingers on the last step, watching us in grim silence.
His sharp nose punctures the protective sheath of our sad
gathering.

I try to summon a firm voice. "Good morning, Mr. Abbey."

"And a good morning to you," Abbey replies, placing his
spectacles in the pocket of his vest. He regards us all from a
strange, neutral distance, his lips set tightly together like bars
of metal. "My condolences to all of you."

We thank him in our various ways.

Fanny has wandered over to a gleaming metal object that rests on a table off to the side of the room. It consists of two pans hung from a horizontal lever. "It's so pretty!" she exclaims.

Abbey's brow wrinkles. "Whether or not it is pretty is a matter of little consequence," he informs her. "That device is a double-pan balance. We use it to measure out exact quantities of tea."

"Surely its charming symmetry—its prettiness—is related to its utility, and is therefore inseparable from its function," I point out.

Abbey lets out a faint snort. "Perhaps. But a more mature way of viewing it would be to consider, instead, the lessons it teaches for a moderate life. As we become adults, we must learn to check our natural impulses and keep our lives in balance."

Fanny has tilted her head to the side. "Are our natural impulses wrong?" she asks.

"Almost always," is the immediate reply. "At the end of our lives, we each face a much larger and more forbidding balance scale—the judgment of the Lord. Those who obey His laws on earth will find eternal life."

Tom starts to laugh; I give him a look, and he turns it into a cough.

Abbey's eyes rest on my nicely pressed work jacket. "How goes your surgical apprenticeship?"

I take a moment to frame my response. "I'm glad you asked. There are some new developments. I will need to speak to you sometime in the near future."

Abbey's upper lip curls ever so slightly. He turns and plods back up the stairs, one spare step at a time.

≈✥✥✥≈

Half obscured by Abbey's ringing footfalls is Fanny's whispered plea: "Don't let them force me to live with them. Please, John! It will be the death of me!"

At the time I missed her entreaty, so distracted was I by my own concerns. After several years of medical training I'd come to a crossroads, and the choice I faced in the next year weighed on my mind, full of hazard.

The scalpel or the pen?

A safe and prosperous life or an embrace of poverty?

A well-traveled highway or a plunge into the wilderness?

My choice was ill-advised. It was rash. I told myself then that it was a brave act—the most courageous thing I could do. And after that, there was no going back. Poetry was all.

No matter whom I left behind.

N

Raven man's hollow footfalls still echoed in the air, but the surroundings melted away. Factories gave way to slate-roofed houses set in spacious gardens and groves of oak and maple. Black smoke yielded to grey banks of fog and mist.

There he was again, his angular body padding through a comfortable room toward a high-backed chair. As he seated himself, a surprising change took place. His hair grew white in a flash like grass in a deep frost, gullies formed in his cheeks, and folds of skin gathered under his chin. His shoulders bent forward.

Outside, a man approached the house in jerky bursts like the flight of a swallow—a few steps, pause, a few more steps, pause. He wore baggy trousers and a loose, ill-fitting coat that gave him the look of a starving cat. In his left arm, he carried a small bundle.

He stopped at the front door and glanced toward the sky for no reason I could see. Something—worry? the passing of years?—had creased a line across the center of his forehead.

It was the poet.

J

Abbey's spectacles glint when the servant ushers me into the parlor, and I can't tell what emotion they conceal.

He lowers his head to size me up over the top of them, and now I see that a frown pulls down every feature of his face—brow, cheeks, mouth—with displeasure.

"And to what do we owe the honor?" His lips part, as if tasting something unsavory.

"I have come to see Fanny."

"It's been a while, hasn't it? I wasn't sure she still had an eldest brother."

I am a vessel in danger of spilling. "I am here to make up for my absence. And also, of course, to pay my respects to you and Mrs. Abbey."

The spectacles glance toward the ceiling. "Mrs. Abbey will survive perfectly well without your respects. As will Fanny. She is recovering from an illness and is not able to accept visitors."

"I am not a 'visitor.' She is my sister."

"Well, so we are told."

Heat rushes into my face.

Abbey lets out a sigh. "Be seated. I will see if she is well enough to come down." He calls over a servant and speaks quietly to her.

A few minutes later, escorted by Mrs. Abbey, Fanny appears in the doorway, a bit flushed, dressed in her nightgown. A smile brightens her face as she sees me, and she dances over and throws her arms around me.

"Oh, John, I had no idea you were coming!" She brushes away her tears as if annoyed by them. "Why has it been so long?"

To say I have devoted every second of my existence for the past year to poetry is no excuse, but it is all I have to offer. "My second volume of verse required a bit more attention than I counted on." I hand a book to her. "This is for you," I whisper. "I suspect Mr. Abbey hasn't shared his copy with you."

She holds the book before her and gazes lovingly at the title. "Oh, John, thank you! What does 'Endymion' mean?"

"He's a Greek shepherd, beloved of the moon—"

"Enough of this nonsense!" As dried and stringy as old hemp, Mrs. Abbey minces over and peers down at us.

"It's not nonsense!" Fanny protests.

"I will overlook your impertinence, if you rein yourself in."

"Impertinence? But Mrs. Abbey—"

Mrs. Abbey shakes a finger at Fanny. "You're in a state of unnatural excitement from the sudden appearance of your brother. I never thought I'd see a Keats move so quickly across the room." Her thin lips stretch apart like inchworms. "They were ever indolent—and will ever be so. It was born in them, I believe."

Fanny's lips press up to my ear. "Well," she whispers, "if it is born in us, how can we help it?"

I cough to hide my laughter.

"And what is it that we find so amusing?" Mr. Abbey asks.

"It's nothing," I reply, taking Fanny's hand and swinging it back and forth.

"Nothing?"

"Nothing."

"How fitting that you used that word," Abbey observes.

I raise my head and give him an inquiring look.

"It reminds me of something I read recently. A book of poetry," he snickers.

"Would you care to explain what you mean?" I find myself forced to ask.

An expression ripples across his face. "Well, John, I have read your book and it reminds me of the Quaker's horse which was hard to catch and good for nothing when he was caught. So your book is hard to understand and good for nothing when it is understood."

Fanny makes a little sound like a trapped animal. "How dare you!" she cries. "How dare you insult John so!"

"That's more than enough from you, young lady." Mrs. Abbey wrenches her away so abruptly that Fanny has no time to put up any resistance.

"Back to bed with you," she commands. With sinewy strength, she drags Fanny out the door to the stairwell as the stunned girl clutches the book to her chest.

Fanny's voice, half muffled, calls from behind the door. "Don't listen to them, John!"

Abbey spreads his hands apart like someone who believes he has the power to calm the world or soothe agitated waters. "John, you're old enough by now to understand that the truth—the unvarnished truth—is the best medicine for what ails you. But don't just take my word for it. Earlier this evening,

I happened upon someone else's thoughts on your work." He holds up the magazine. "*Blackwood's*. A reputable publication, is it not?"

"It's a Tory publication that thinks poetry should be the plaything of nobility," I reply.

Abbey opens the magazine and reads aloud with evident pleasure. "'It is a better and a wiser thing to be a starved apothecary than a starved poet; so back to the shop Mr John, back to the plasters, pills, and ointment boxes. But be a little more sparing of soporifics in your practice than you have been in your poetry.'" He sits back and cracks his knuckles.

Tilting my head, I detect the soft footfall of steps behind the door to the stairs.

"Well?" Abbey asks. "Have you nothing to say for yourself?"

I don't bite.

"Really?" Abbey prods. "No reaction at all?"

I cross my arms. "I am a more severe critic of my own works than anyone else could ever be."

"Do you intend to continue your career as a poet?" he purrs.

I nod.

"And what are your expectations, may I ask?"

"That I shall be among the English poets after my death."

Abbey lets out a long and jagged laugh that ends with a burst of gasps like someone choking on a piece of beef. "Simply astonishing!" he exclaims. "Surely you are the only person in the world who could possibly believe such an absurdity."

"Mock me as you wish, Mr. Abbey. I have no doubt there is good reason to do so. But I have come on other business."

A smirk flashes across his face. "Very well. Proceed."

I take a deep breath. "Mr. Abbey, this is a matter of grave concern. Tom is ill. His condition is serious. I would like to secure your permission for Fanny to visit him." I test an entreating look.

Abbey's mouth sets primly. "Shall I recall for you what happened when I allowed a visit last spring?"

"It was a perfectly good visit."

Abbey shakes his head. "It was no such thing."

"What was wrong?"

"You introduced your innocent young sister to the society of some highly unsavory men. Fanny told us all about it herself, in great detail." The voice is both smug and accusatory. "She said the men took shocking liberties with her."

The door to the staircase bursts open, and Fanny stands before us. "I said no such thing!" she declares. Splotches of red stain her face.

Abbey turns his astonished spectacles toward the girl.

"Fanny!" I caution her.

"It's a lie!" she insists. "It's all a lie. Everything he says is a lie!"

"Young lady, you were ordered to go to your room." Abbey brandishes a bony finger toward the upstairs; Fanny crosses her arms and refuses to move.

Every ounce of my being wants to take her side, but what good can that do? I imagine the consequences if she carries her rebellion any further.

"Fanny—do as Mr. Abbey says. Please!" I implore her.

She casts a withering look in my direction, throws her arms up in the air, and stomps up the stairs.

"Some brother you are!" echoes her voice from the stairwell.

I take another deep breath. "I apologize for the outburst."

Abbey lifts an eyebrow. "You see what comes of giving her too much license. No one will ever want to marry such a headstrong young thing." His lips smack slightly. "As for your request, her visit is denied."

I rise, give a stiff bow, and let myself out before the servant can intercede.

⁂

It's so easy—*now*—to see how I hid my doubt and uncertainty behind a cloak of pride, fancying that a stiff bow was a gesture of strength.

What a failure I was. I failed Tom. I failed Fanny. I failed to protect either of them from the dangers that stalked them.

I buried the truth of my shortcomings beneath shovelfuls of activity—in writing and in seeking recognition. During those years, I was so intent on how I would define myself to the world: the self-assured artist, securing the approval of the great ones who went before him.

Self-assured indeed.

I turn to the spirit, throw my arms into the air in a gesture of futility, and offer a grimace that is meant as an apology for my failings. As if an apology to this curious creature can be of any use.

Alarmed by the sudden motion, the spirit flits off into the dusk.

N

I soon returned. For reasons I didn't understand, I had to stay with him.

I could now recognize one type of pain that the poet felt: regret. He regretted many of his past actions, in particular his dealings with his sister and brothers. Birds sometimes experience something similar. There was a robin I once observed, on a summer day so perfect it was easy to forget that danger never shuts its eyes. Flying off in search of food for her children, she spied a pool of water on the ground and fluttered onto a nearby rock. After a few quick glances around her, she hopped into the pool and began to clean herself, dipping her wings in the water and shaking them in the warmth of the sun.

But in the short time she took to groom herself, a squirrel crept down from the highest branches of her oak tree, silent and deadly, and approached her nest of fledglings.

From my perch in the plum tree I chirped, whistled, and buzzed to warn her of the danger. She must have thought it nothing but typical nightingale chatter. She dipped her wings again and shook herself dry, then repeated the process two more times.

I shot off through the mild summer air directly toward the oak tree and swished by the squirrel in warning, distant enough to avoid its brutal claws but close enough to see the murderous glint in its eyes.

My warning flight only caused the villain to redouble the speed of its approach.

By now, the mother had completed her bath and lifted herself into the air to ride the gentle wind currents back home. She glided up to the nest, rose above it, and beat her wings furiously. A squawk. Several harsher squawks. A series of shrieks. The flurry of attack.

The squirrel scurried to the end of a branch, leaped across the void to a maple tree, and scrambled off into the greenery.

The mother returned to her nest, and there followed a series of stricken cries.

What I felt then was regret. If not for my warning flight—which quickened the arrival of the squirrel—the mother robin might have returned in time to save a fledgling or two.

Has the word been invented for the loss she felt then? Her mate returned and they mourned together. It was a pain too great to bear alone.

The earthbound do not own their lives separately. They are bound in pain with the lives of those around them. Just as we are, who flock with family or friends in good times and bad.

Yet humans regard their lives in ways that are perplexing. Even in the midst of pain—horrible pain—they seem to expect to find something. Something larger or greater. During his life, the poet clung to the thought "That I shall be among the English poets after my death." A senseless goal, and only now was the poet beginning to understand how blind it was.

As I watch and listen to humans, I begin to see that the earthbound hope to gain something by their ceaseless struggles. They believe there is more to their lives than merely dwelling in the moment. It strikes me as folly.

What exactly could that "something more" be? That is the mystery of their lives.

Could this mystery be connected in some way to the tug I feel in my heart? It tells me to remain near the poet, as if there is something he needs from me.

My feelings are less tangled than the mix of sorrow and pain and hope that flood through the lives of humans.

But I have begun to appreciate the richness in the voice of the poet—the phrases I overhear, the poems I hear him recite—at times a brightness like the cry of the whippoorwill, at other times a shadow like the mourning of a dove.

And I've discovered another connection between us. Oddly, it was the poet's words to Raven man: *I mean to rely upon my abilities as a poet.*

Those brave words remind me of the splendor of flight.

J

Some brother you are.

Fanny's words sting like a splinter that enters your flesh and works its way toward your heart.

That is, if you have a heart … which I don't anymore, thanks to Mr. Abbey.

There is a strange symmetry here. I am trapped in this way station, this seemingly endless void. But the void within is even greater.

N

Words are like the taunts of a blue jay, but more cutting and subtle. By sharpening the edges of their words, the earthbound have refined the delivery of pain.

Some words seem to bring terror; it's in their very nature.

Death.

A terrifying word, like the shriek of an owl on a moonless night, perhaps.

Nightingales live innocent of this terror. When one departs, there are others to carry on. The loss is hardly remarked.

But the earthbound live with death hanging around their

necks every second of their lives—the knowledge that all this will come to an end.

The poet, of course, knew death all too well. His father, his mother. His grandparents. His brother.

He seemed to see poetry as a form of combat meant to wrestle death into the dust so he could rid himself of it forever.

But each day of his life, death peered over his shoulder.

IV

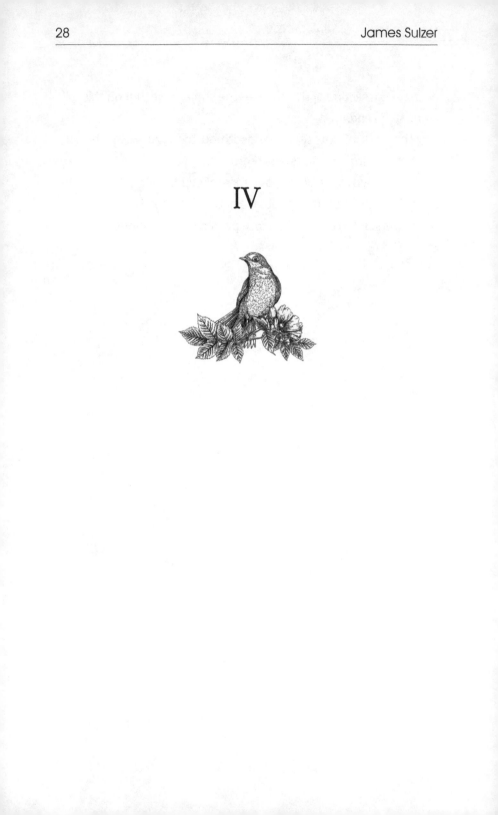

N

From the darkness, the bed floated into view again with the young man called Tom, pale as bone, stretched upon it.

The reason for his color soon became clear. He was, in fact, nothing but bones—a skeleton feathered over in the clothes of a man. The stubs of his fingers jutted out from his shirtsleeve like bits of straw from an abandoned nest.

John, have you forgotten me?

J

I turn my head. I have the sensation of having wolfed down a meal that is too rich to digest. The dark mass in the belly. The heaviness just before you stagger from the room, fall onto your knees, and wait for the horror of your excesses to spew forth.

N

The ground beneath us crackled several times and hatched open.

Rows of boys seated at desks. The pale boy near the back of the room fidgeted in his seat, drawing pictures of cats with his chalk and piece of slate. A heavyset man strode up to him, and the boy screwed up his eyes to meet his.

"You're Tom Keats, the new boy?" the man asked.

Tom nodded.

"How are you getting on with your work?"

"As well as I wish," he replied.

The man ground his fist into his other hand. "As well as you wish?"

"I don't much fancy the work they give you here."

"*You don't fancy the work?*" The man's eyes glared like the eyes of a fish. "Did you say *you don't fancy the work?*"

Tom shrugged. "You heard me."

"It don't matter if you *fancy* it or not. Now shut your trap and get down to it," the man growled. He slapped the palm of his hand down on the desk.

Tom crossed his arms. "I don't have to listen to you. You're not even a teacher. You're only an usher."

"You'll listen to me or else!" the man shouted. The room had grown quiet; the other students had stopped their work. The usher raised his head and glared at them, and they ducked back down.

"You're nothing more than a common butcher, just like your father." Tom's voice filled the room like the burble of a pheasant.

The man spun toward him. "Only a common butcher, am I?" He paused a moment. "So what if I'm a butcher? Your mother was a slut."

"What did you call my mother?"

"I said your mother was a slut."

"You're a bloody damn liar—"

There was a yelp of pain. Tom bent over, clasping a hand to his ear. The man glowered down at him, his hands on his hips.

An older boy, seated across the room, looked up from his book. He had thick chestnut hair, hazel eyes, and a very wide mouth with an upper lip that protruded slightly over the lower. He stood and turned toward Tom, saw the tears running down his face. The usher flicked his finger against Tom's cheek and swore at him for being such a little girl.

The older boy closed his book. Across its front, letters spelled out the title *A Dictionary of Greek Mythology.* He hurried to the other boy.

"What happened, Tom?" he asked.

Tom rubbed his ear. "He struck me. And John, he said our mother was a slut."

The poet tipped his head toward the usher. "Is that true?"

"*Is that true?* Everyone knows it's true." The usher cleared his throat and spat a glob of rotten egg onto the floor. "Your mother chased after anything that could pull on a pair o' britches."

The poet held out his right palm and spat on it. "Our mother is resting peacefully in her grave. You have no right to speak of her like that."

A laugh. "Look who thinks he can order me about like a gen'lman. You ain't even five foot tall. I'll say what I like, little man."

"We'll see about that." The poet thrust one leg forward, fists cocked. The usher towered over him; he had legs like fence posts and shoulders as broad as a horse cart. As the usher crossed his massive arms and glowered down, the poet took a step forward and threw a punch into his midsection.

The usher grunted and exclaimed, "You little shit! You're asking for it, you are." He clenched his fist and drew back his arm.

The poet hopped back and forth, knees bent. The other children began to gather round at a distance. "It's David and Goliath!" one of them exclaimed.

The usher reached back and threw a huge punch ... and whiffed.

The poet hopped in closer, cheered on by the children.

"I won't miss you this time." The usher reached back for another blow.

"STOP!" The cry resounded through the room.

Everyone froze.

Dust trickled down from the rafters.

An old man with a white wreath of hair stepped into the room, pressing his cane before him.

"Go to your seats, all of you!" he commanded in a ringing voice.

"Yes, Mr. Clark," came the chorus of voices.

There was a pause. "You too!" Mr. Clark ordered the poet in a slightly different tone—still firm, but softer.

Biting his lip, the poet returned to his seat and picked up his book.

"And you," Mr. Clark said, indicating the usher, "you come with me."

The usher shuffled out of the room.

After a glance toward Tom, the poet opened his book and disappeared into its pages like an osprey diving into a lake.

J

Misery and loyalty were the twin channel markers of those dark waters where my soul had begun to sound the depths.

N

The schoolhouse melted in a wave of light. Out of the shimmer rose a simple stone house. An open window on the second floor offered a view into a room.

A figure barely out of boyhood was sprawled on a bed. His eyes were dull, and his face was pale and very thin. He could barely lift an arm in greeting to the young man who appeared at the door, dressed in the ill-fitting coat.

"Is that you, John?"

"Yes, Tom."

"I wondered when you would ever return to Hampstead."

The poet hurried to the bed and fell onto one knee beside it. "I meant to come back sooner. Wordsworth was in London. I stayed there an extra week to meet him."

"You met Wordsworth?"

"Yes." The poet brushed back Tom's hair. "Tom ..." he paused. "You look—"

"Like a ghost," Tom finished for him in a faint voice.

The poet placed his hand on his brother's arm.

"I have my good days and my bad days," Tom whispered. He leaned back and allowed his eyes to close. "This is one of the bad."

The poet found a handkerchief and wiped the blood-specked phlegm off his brother's upper lip.

"Have they been giving you enough to eat?"

"Yes." Tom gestured toward his chest. "But some days I have trouble keeping it down."

"We have to help you get better."

"It will happen," Tom mumbled.

"It must."

"I don't want to be a burden, John."

"You will never be a burden."

"I can feel myself improving."

The poet pursed his lips. "I have to be sure of that before ..." He didn't finish his thought.

"Before what?" Tom asked.

"It's ... just an idea a friend and I have."

"Tell me, John."

"It's my friend Charles Brown." The poet glanced off to the side. "He wants to take a hike through the Lake District—Wordsworth country." His eyes returned to Tom. "But I don't think this is the time to leave you."

Tom produced a smile. "Don't be silly. Mrs. Bentley can watch me."

"She's your landlord, not your nurse."

"She gives me what I need. Food. Attention when I need it. Most days are better than this. John, is it important for you—this trip?"

The poet nodded and his eyes grew distant. "I have a feeling that I shall never learn poetry until I visit the Lakes."

"Then you simply must go."

The poet turned and gazed out the window. "I will check with Brown to see if the offer still holds." Just then, a hawk swooped across the treetops.

A grey day blew in, and two men trudged side by side across a lawn. One was the poet. The other was older and bald.

The dull glare of the sky reduced the pupils of their eyes to grains of black rice.

"The plan is to hike due north, through the Lake Country, and into Scotland," the man recited. "With a side trip to Ireland, if possible." They were striding in the direction of my plum tree— though somehow I knew I was not yet alive.

"Mr. Brown, that sounds like a splendid hike," the poet murmured. "Absolutely splendid."

"You are interested, no doubt, in making the acquaintance of the scenic hills and lakes that have so inspired William Wordsworth," Brown observed.

"I am," the poet confirmed. "Seeing—experiencing—that landscape has become my passion." He gazed off into the distance—but his eyes clouded over, and he sighed.

A brown bird flitted by, then returned for another, closer pass. The poet glanced toward the sky.

As he marched them through some bushes and closer to the tree, Brown held up his hands to frame its stout trunk. He turned to the poet. "I want you to observe the bark of my plum tree—the way it cracks into exquisite little diamond patterns almost like the scales of a big—"

He gave a surprised grunt as if he felt himself being shoved roughly to the side.

(At the same moment, I felt a shudder at the core of my being. Was it because I was watching them tread so close to my plum tree, sometime before my own life took flight? But why then, why at that precise moment?)

By the time Brown regained his balance, the poet had turned away and was facing someone entirely new: a young lady who strolled easy as a partridge across the grass in their direction. She wore the leaf-colored dress.

"Do grown men have nothing better to do than jostle each other about like little children?" she called.

Brown pivoted toward her. "Oh, hello, Miss Brawne."

She stopped short of them. "Good day, Mr. Brown. Who is your violent young friend?"

"John Keats, the poet," Brown said.

"The poet and pugilist, it seems," she added, with a twist of her mouth.

"He is thinking of accompanying me on my hike north this summer, while your family rents my flat."

"You may want to reconsider that," she advised him. "It seems quite possible he might knock you off a mountaintop for sport and watch you topple down the slope."

The poet drew his hands apart and opened his mouth, but he seemed unable to give voice to his thoughts. He was having trouble taking a breath.

Brown and Miss Brawne spent a few minutes in quiet discussion. "Your mother will have the lease within a day," he assured her, and after a final glance at the poet, she took her leave.

"Who is that bewitching young woman?" the poet asked in a quiet voice.

"Oh, that's Fanny Brawne. Her family is renting my half of Wentworth Place. She's all right," Brown informed him.

"She's much more than that."

"I can't say she gained a very good first impression of *you*," Brown told him. "What the hell were you thinking, giving me a shove like that?"

"Oh, that. Well ..." The poet's eyes were on Fanny Brawne as she disappeared around the side of the house, and his voice trailed off to silence.

J

The vistas are more varied and spacious and lovely than I imagined—than I could possibly have imagined. Immense silver lakes flood to the rim of the distant horizon, shimmering beneath a stately succession of sun and shadow. Brilliant green fields, dotted with dark-faced Herdwick sheep, lift and fall in swells and folds and meet in charming angles at rugged stone walls. Pale sage mountains rise in stunning vertical sweeps, crack open into deep chasms and flinty cliffs, and soar off into the clouds. A beauty of a more humble kind spreads itself at our feet. Ferns festoon the forest floors with tangled exuberance. A flower known as foxglove grows everywhere—tall, glowing torches of purple or yellow—flourishing beside the paths, even taking root in outcroppings of slate. Fog and mist descend in a moment from nowhere and wrap the muted world in a blanket of silken mystery. I write to Tom that the tone, the coloring, the slate, the moss, the rockweed all astonish me; the place has an intellect, a countenance all its own. Here, I know, I shall learn poetry.

N

From a fair height above the earth we observed the snail's pace of their hike—from one town to the next, past lakes, across mountain ranges. They moved north of the waters and entered a rockier, hillier, drier land. There the hike came to an end.

We were back at the simple stone house with the open window in a second-story room.

J

When I step into Tom's room in the rented house at Well Walk, Mrs. Bentley clasps her hands to her chest and withdraws without a word.

Lying in Tom's bed is a shriveled-up old man with sunken cheeks, sticks for arms, and masses of wrinkles about his skinny neck.

"Oh, dear God!" I kneel beside the bed and grasp Tom's left hand between my own. It feels as thin as paper and almost as weightless.

Tom's head rotates toward me, and his pale eyes give a flicker of recognition. His throat swells as if he is about to speak, but he cannot. He turns away and coughs, and a fine spray of blood spatters the pillow.

"My darling Tom." I jump up, grab a cloth, and wipe a stream of bloody phlegm from his face and throat. "I will never leave you again."

For the next months after my return from the Lake District, I care for Tom night and day. I rarely leave his bed. But it is not enough to save him.

Or me, I suspect.

𝒩

Then we were alone in the twilight. But not for long, for once again the bed drifted toward us, bathed in a glow as soft as a bank of sunlit fog, feathering a valley on an autumn morning. The skeleton of the poet's brother had returned, lying on his back, his hands crossed on his chest.

Tom, I knew better. I knew I shouldn't go. Can you ever forgive me?
The light broadened over the bed.

I was a fool. I listened with my ears instead of my heart. Is there no way I can alter the misdeeds of my past?
The poet raised his head to the heavens.

J

The silence that answers is all too clear. The past is immutable; nothing can be changed. The suffering we caused. The hopes we blighted. The loyalty we betrayed.

The pain we carry forward is the price we pay, and I suspect it can never dissolve. We can only try to understand what led us to hurt those most dear to us.

I wonder. Is it possible to submit these fragments of our lives—our deeds and our misdeeds—to the impartial judgment of the universe?

Again I raise my head toward the heavens.

N

The poet looked up, as if trying to contact some power lurking in the darkness, a large and invisible owl, or a grey heron too subtle and sly to let itself be seen. And then he spoke.

J

I would like to submit the record of my actions with my brother Tom to the wisdom of the universe and await its judgment.

N

No sooner had he said the words than the bed faded away and a pale cloud appeared in the western sky. Inside the cloud, two dark, motionless figures faced each other in profile. Their arms were cocked and their fists clenched, ready to fight. One of the figures was giant and the other was small, barely larger than a child.

The usher—and me.

From the eastern sky drifted a second cloud that bore the image of a window frame through which could be seen the back of a traveler striding off down a road.

There I am, departing on my hike to the Lake District. Naughty boy. The ratty old jacket—the scruffy boots. The knapsack. My outfit exactly.

Then the starlight was blocked out by something strange.

J

A double-pan balance such as tea merchants use, but of immense size, towers over us higher than the greatest chestnut tree, casting a dazzling light like the reflection of sunlight off water. In this gloom, it radiates a severe authority and the terrible inevitability of the judgment I requested.

In its presence, the elements of my troubled past seem to know their places. Each cloud floats over to a weighing pan and settles upon it—the duo of pugilists on the left pan, the image of the window and traveler on the right. My loyalty toward Tom on the one side, my neglect of him on the other.

N

Which was greater—the poet's loyalty on the left, or his neglect? For a moment, the pans tipped up and down like a seesaw.

And settled lower on the right—significantly lower.

The poet whispered, *So it is determined. In this aspect of my life, I failed.*

Then a third cloud floated into view and made its way toward the balance scale. This cloud held Tom lying in his bed in his final days and the silhouette of the poet kneeling beside it.

The poet watched silently as the cloud bumped its way onto the balance pan on the left and snuggled in next to the pugilists.

Slowly but steadily, the left balance pan sank like a falling tide—and almost evened out the difference. But not quite. The left pan still hovered a feather's breadth above the pan on the right.

The poet bowed his head.

J

Whether this is all the creation of my own mind—conjured by my doubts and regrets—or whether it indeed springs from the wisdom of the universe and the vastness of the night, the balance scale has decided against me.

N

The poet remained bent like a willow branch in an ice storm.

Darling Tom, I hope you can forgive me. I hold you in my heart forever.

The balance scale and the cloud images faded into the bed, bathed in a pale rose light, with Tom motionless upon it, his hands still crossed on his chest—his flesh restored to him, but not his life.

A girl flowed in and touched the poet's hand, and he stood up.

Is that Tom?

Yes, Fanny, replied the poet. Would you care to look upon him?

I must. I must see him once more. Oh, John, he looks calm. In the end, I think our brother is at peace.

The poet turned to face her.

Fanny, I—I need to request your forgiveness.

Forgiveness? For what, John?

For being absent. For being away so long, from you—and from Tom. For not giving you both the love you needed.

Those were hard times, John. For all of us.

It doesn't excuse my actions.

I do have one question, John. When I cried out for you in my time of deepest need, when I sent the note that I was in crisis with the Abbeys, did you try to come?

I tried to, Fanny. I ran outside to hail a stagecoach, but at that moment a rush of blood came to my throat—the worst I had experienced to that point. I had no choice but to stumble back inside and collapse on my bed.

Oh, John.

A doctor was summoned, and he confirmed my worst fears. Consumption. Soon after I was sent off to Italy.

So when Abbey told me you had no interest in visiting me, he was lying?

Of course he was lying.

The truth is, there was no way you could have come.

Not then. But I have no excuse for not coming earlier.

John, you did what you could. No one can do more.

He pressed her hand.

In the many ways I failed you, I ask for your forgiveness, and I offer you the full measure of my love.

She placed her hands on his shoulders.

You have my forgiveness, and more importantly, dear John, you have my love. She gave him a peck on the cheek.

And for now, I bid you adieu.

The light around the bed grew still and cold like moonlight frosting a wisp of cloud, and the bed and the girl dissolved into the darkness.

N

Raven man drifted back into view, dwarfed by his great desk. The lenses of his spectacles glinted in the light of a single candle. Scratching the tip of his pen on the paper, he jotted some figures, bent forward, tilted his head to one side, smacked his lips, and scratched some more.

The poet floated over behind the desk and peered down at a pile of papers. He looked over one page, then a second, and a third—and then he picked up the entire packet and flung it aside.

And so the truth finally comes out, said the poet.

Kindly treat my personal papers with respect.

Those papers appear to be a secret inventory of the ways you invested my grandfather's estate—and it was all for your own purposes. Buildings, land, even a merchant ship bound for Jamaica!

Raven man shook a bag half full of silver coins.

You might have known this all along, if you hadn't been such a fool.

Slender beams of angry yellow light shot out of the poet's chest toward Raven man—who batted them away with the back of his hand. The shafts of light piled up in a little nest and turned ash grey.

All this time, every miserable day, you were defrauding us.

Such a discovery should stir your youthful blood and quicken your pulse. But dear me, aren't you missing something necessary to the task?

What are you talking about?

Isn't that your heart down there on the floor, encrusted with mouse droppings?

You are monstrous.

No more so than you, with your monstrous conceit that you shall one day be numbered among the English poets.

The poet reached forward and knocked the pen out of his claw.

What do you know of the viewless wings of poesy?

Raven man bent forward calmly to retrieve his pen.

It must be infuriating for you to finally understand the true depths of your failure!

He drifted off into the gloom, a smile frozen on his face.

✳️⟨ᄃᄃᄃ⟩✳️

I knew Raven man was using words that were designed to hurt the poet—words like *monstrous conceit* and *infuriating*. Their exact meanings escaped me, but in his voice there was something of the shamelessness of a vulture.

Why do humans expect to find beauty in their lives? How is it possible to rise high enough to perceive beauty when you are bound to the ground by two thick legs?

The young man said he could take flight on the viewless wings of poesy.

Poesy ... another new word. A species of bird whose feathers, it may be, are composed of words.

✳️⟨ᄃᄃᄃ⟩✳️

Once again, they rolled out of the gloom in single file, three grown men straddling their skinny little wheeled vehicles. Pounding their feet beneath them, they thrust themselves toward the poet. He sat gazing into the distance.

At the approach of their buzzing wheels, he looked up and recoiled. But he straightened his back and awaited their arrival.

Again they stopped just short of his face.

Uneducated Cockney!

You have no justification to be angry with us, dear boy. We tried to save you by wholesome and severe discipline.

Did you really believe that Wordsworth, the purest, loftiest, and most classical of poets, should consort with a Cockney poetaster?

And once again, in perfect unison, they each raised a leg and unleashed their loathsome liquid upon the poet, then stomped off on their wheeled mounts.

⁕⁓⁞⊙⁞⁓⁕

The poet brushed himself off and sat up, a look upon his face that I could not read.

Did he still believe that suffering can reveal its own wisdom, equal perhaps even to that of joy?

Strange opposites to lay side by side in the nest of one's life.

J

Whatever suffering visits me is no more than I deserve. The universe has already rendered one judgment against me. There may be more to follow.

Beside me, the light pulses.

Spirit, is this another sign of sympathy from you? Or perhaps alarm? Who are you, and why do you linger by my side?

Do you take pleasure in my humiliation at the hands (or other bodily parts) of my critics?

$\mathcal{N}$

If I had a voice, my answers would be: Yes, I feel both—sympathy and alarm. No, I don't take pleasure in your humiliation. And I linger by your side for reasons I still don't understand.

It's as if I had a debt to this human poet.

I know I met with him once, when he sat beneath my tree and his hand began to make words on paper. Could there have been another time?

When I was still a fledgling, huddled in the nest beside my brother and sister, a young man went about the yard, spewing a loud string of sounds, and didn't I tremble at the fearsome roar?

I only saw the top of his head. His dark hair was thick like lamb's wool.

My mother alighted then, and she let it be known by warbles and whistles and looks in his direction, accompanied by the unhurried refolding of her wings, that there was no reason to be worried. She perched unafraid and unruffled as he passed close by our nest, a sign that this large and loud human was, in fact, our true friend—maybe the best we would find among the earthbound. But she never revealed why.

⁂

Something larger than an eyrie floated toward us, trailed by a cloud of golden flowers that rippled like the waves of a lake.

Resting upon it, his head propped up on pillows, lay a man dressed in an open-collared shirt and plain brown breeches. His white hair had been combed up and onto his bald head, giving him a crown like a baby eagle.

The poet looked up and saw the man and knelt before him.

Good evening, Mr. Keats.

Good evening, Mr. Wordsworth.

I take it that you kneel to honor the humble beauty of my daffodils.

To be sure, the host of daffodils is as striking in person as in your beloved lyric. But the truth is, I am in dread and wonder at the prospect of meeting you. You have no idea how inspiring your verse has been to me.

Please, stand up. And pray recite for me a piece of your verse.

The poet rose to his feet.

I will be honored. Um—this is one of my early works.

Oh? How long ago did you compose it?

A few months.

Wordsworth wrinkled his lofty brow. *Very well. Does it come with a title?*

It is my "Hymn to Pan." From *Endymion.*

The poet paced back and forth and recited:

> Oh thou, whose mighty palace roof doth hang
> From jagged trunks, and overshadoweth
> Eternal whispers, glooms, the birth, life, death
> Of unseen flowers in heavy peacefulness;
> Who lov'st to see the hamadryads dress
> Their ruffled locks where meeting hazels darken—

Wordsworth held up a hand. *Thank you.*

But—there's more. Many lines more. Hundreds, in fact.

It is sufficient.

What—what is your opinion of my verse?

A very pretty piece of paganism.

The last word struck the poet like a blow to the face.

I see.

Wordsworth leaned forward and jabbed an index finger. *Remember that simplicity is a virtue. As is emotion—within limits, of course—emotion recollected in tranquility.*

Yes. Yes, I see.

Now I must leave my couch and direct the full power of my genius to my correspondence with the deputy comptroller of stamps.

The couch and Wordsworth drifted away, followed by the crowd of golden daffodils.

J

How I longed to be recognized, even early on, when my verse was a leap headlong into the sea. Years before I was ready. Years before my time.

The truth is, my time will never come.

I am John Keats, a man of little knowledge and middling intellect.

N

Poets seem to dwell in words as a nightingale dwells in trees and bushes. Which means, above all, that poets must know the worth of their words, their words' worth.

Wordsworth. A fitting name for a poet—or is it, perhaps, too perfect? Like a cuckoo's egg, a spot-on replica of the sparrow hawk's?

Words must have as many facets as the eyes of a dragonfly. They can be kind, but they can also be fierce weapons.

A very pretty piece of paganism.

The cause of breathless shock and a wound deep and raw.

⁂

A spacious room opened beneath us, full of bright colors and steeply slanted desks and sticks of various sizes with soft grass tips. These were all jumbled in a heap to one side. A long table, covered with fruits and dishes and bottles, filled the center of the room.

High on the wall behind the table shone a bearded man in a white robe, astride a donkey that didn't move, surrounded by a crowd of men who didn't move, including one who looked like the poet. The wall had captured them as a pool of water captures a tree that soars into the sky above its still surface.

J

The "Immortal Dinner"! How well I recall it! The date is etched on my soul: December 28, 1817. And the guest list: William Wordsworth, his cousin Thomas Monkhouse, the amiable jokester Charles Lamb, and a little-known poet, John Keats (myself, that is).

And one fateful guest who would arrive in secret.

N

Pigeon man stood inside the room, facing the door. As each guest entered, he and his belly tipped forward as if about to scratch the ground for food. Last to arrive was the poet, who hopped into the room, bright-eyed and smiling.

J

What a scene greets me as I enter Haydon's studio! Artists, poets, revelry, food, wine from the Bordeaux! The immense canvas of Haydon's unfinished painting *Christ's Entry into Jerusalem* looms over us all. I sneak a look, delighted to see the profile of my face on the canvas, directly above the bowed head of William Wordsworth—a generous gesture by Benjamin Haydon, who knows how I worship the great poet.

Haydon, portly and pretentious, is seated at the head of the table, with Wordsworth to his left and Lamb to his right. Monkhouse is beside Wordsworth, and I am beside Lamb (and beside myself with joy).

Wine flows like a mountain stream as the meal commences.

"Why the devil did you include Newton on your canvas?" Lamb remarks to Haydon. "A fellow who believed nothing unless it was as clear as the three sides of a triangle." He holds up his glass of Bordeaux, examines its smoky red hue, and furrows his hairy brow.

My tongue loosened already by the alcohol, I hazard an opinion. "It seems to me that Newton destroyed all the poetry of the rainbow by reducing it to a prism."

Lamb swivels toward me. "Right you are!" he roars. "Right you are! I believe you said it best, William. What's that damned quote of yours about dissecting?"

"We murder to dissect," Wordsworth replies, with a benevolent nod of his bare head. For this dinner, he has put aside his usual rustic attire in favor of knee breeches and a dress shirt with a stiff collar and silk cravat.

He lays down his knife, picks up his fork, and captures a piece of potato.

"That's it!" Haydon exclaims. "That's it in a nutshell, William!" He spears a potato of his own with the air of a warrior who takes no prisoners.

I stand up, holding onto the table to steady myself. "Well, then, since we are in agreement … I drink to Newton's health—and confusion to mathematics!"

"I drink to that gladly!" Wordsworth agrees, eyeing me with a gleam that seems to portend a growing bond of affection. A spasm of warmth shoots through me.

Everyone stands and drinks.

Haydon strolls over and drapes an arm around me. "Do you see what an immense honor I conferred upon you by putting you on that canvas with Wordsworth?"

"Yes. It's … it's wonderful!" I exclaim. The flush of fellowship bathes us in its elixir.

"You're welcome. The bill will come later!" he adds. His comment arrives with the easy familiarity of a joke but lingers in my mind like a threat.

When dinner finally comes to an end, Lamb has collapsed like a sack of coal and appears unable to stir himself. Somehow, he manages to stagger into the front room with the rest of us for tea. In truth, none of us are much better off.

Someone new is in the room, a stranger, dressed in black, seated rigidly upright on one of the couches. The party flows around him like a herd of garrulous seals spreading around a rocky formation on a beach. I take a seat in a chair and hold onto the arms to keep from slipping into the depths of the ocean.

Lamb pours himself onto the couch by the fire and fixes his eyes on the newcomer. He blinks several times. "What is that thing?" he asks Haydon.

Haydon signals Lamb to keep his voice down. "Oh, that would be Kingston. The comptroller of stamps. Wants to meet Wordsworth." Haydon's eyes, which always bulge a bit like the eyes of a pike, now seem ready to pop out of their sockets.

"Meet Wordsworth? What for?" I peep.

Haydon's voice is in my ear. "He's the official who oversees Wordsworth's sinecure. The distributor of stamps for Westmorland. It's a lucrative position and requires no work on Wordsworth's part but overseeing a clerk."

Haydon stands and tries with little success to raise his voice above the clamor and make introductions all around. He finds a spot next to Lamb, who is shaking his head in disbelief.

"Stiff as a board. I'll make him sorry he ever tried to invade our friendly little gathering with his priggish, uh …" Lamb surrenders his body to the couch and falls asleep, his head on Haydon's expansive lap.

The newcomer glances about nervously. He stretches his neck and adjusts his collar. Addressing Wordsworth: "Don't you think, sir, Milton was a great genius?"

Lamb rouses himself from his sleep and cries out, "Pray, sir, did you say Milton was a great genius?"

"No, sir, I asked Mr. Wordsworth if he were not."

"Oh, then you are a silly fellow," Lamb declares. He flops back down.

"Charles, my dear Charles ..." Wordsworth cautions. But Lamb is already asleep again.

The room falls silent.

Kingston tries again in his pinched, nasal voice. "Don't you think Milton was a great genius?"

Wordsworth grimaces and seems to be trying to recall who this astonishing bore might be.

Somehow, Lamb rouses himself again. He stands up, finds a candle, and holds it before him. "Sir, will you allow me to look at your phrenological development?" He stumbles over and examines Kingston's head with mock seriousness and inquires, "What is your given name, sir?"

"John."

"John?" He pauses a moment. "John. Well, yes. That will do."

He turns his back on Kingston, wiggles his posterior, and chants, "Diddle diddle dumpling, my son John, went to bed with his breeches on."

"My dear Charles," Wordsworth declares again.

But Kingston is not to be deterred. In fact, he gives a little chuckle of triumph.

"I have had the honor of some correspondence with you, Mr. Wordsworth."

Wordsworth stares back in chilly silence. "With me, sir? Not that I recall."

Kingston draws himself more erect. "Don't you, sir? I am a comptroller of stamps."

Wordsworth receives the news in stunned silence. This man has the power to dismiss him at any time from his sinecure.

In the ensuing pause, Lamb sings out, "Hey diddle, diddle, the cat and the fiddle."

"Enough, my dear Charles," Wordsworth remonstrates.

Lamb staggers forward and exclaims, "Do let me have another look at that gentleman's organs."

Before Lamb can say or do anything else, Haydon and I push and lug him into the painting studio, where we collapse onto the floor beside him in gales of laughter. But we prop the door open a crack so we can watch the ongoing drama play itself out.

The comptroller's face has turned beet red.

Wordsworth stands, quaking slightly, and gives a formal bow. "Mr. Kingston, I … I beg your pardon for the unforgivable rudeness that you have suffered tonight." He turns in our direction. Through the door he has heard our laughter, and his brow settles into a stern expression.

The comptroller of stamps is also on his feet, standing there like a squirrel that has preened itself for a party.

Kingston addresses Wordsworth one last time. The pinched voice reaches a new and higher register. "Sir, I must say that I am quite unaccustomed to this sort of treatment. Quite unaccustomed. Might I add that I have never experienced anything like it." And with that, he wheels and strides toward the door.

Wordsworth hurries after him and offers some quiet words, inaudible to our ears. No matter, we are dissolving in laughter as we melt down further in the after-flow of wine.

The Immortal Dinner ends soon thereafter. And with it, all my hopes of friendship with the great William Wordsworth.

VI

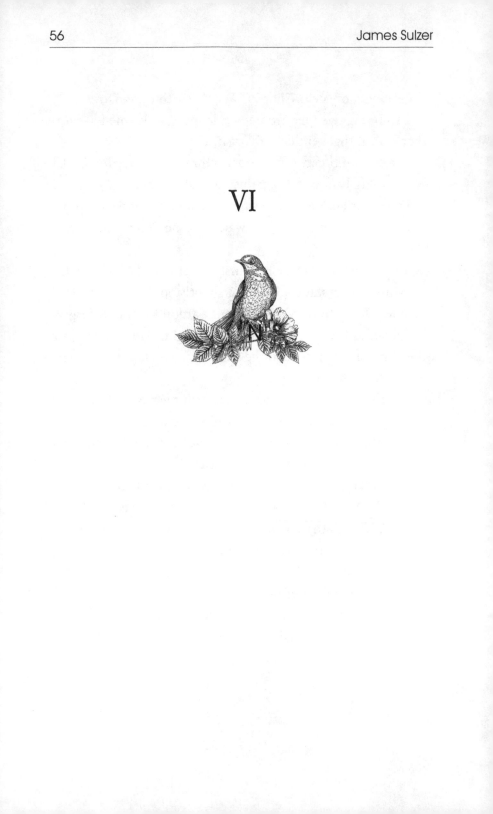

N

We drifted higher above the blue curve of the earth.

The young woman in the dress of leaves flickered up to the poet like a flame and stood with arms crossed before his hunched-over figure.

It wasn't that I didn't love you. It was that you lacked the courage to declare your love for me.

Fanny Brawne, you know that's not true. I declared myself at your mercy. I confessed to you that I cannot live without you.

Actions speak louder than words. You left me again and again.

My love, have you forgotten in my hour of sickness that I stumbled for miles through a frozen landscape, in the grip of a raging fever, in the forlorn hope that I might see you just once more?

Need and love are not the same. Officer?

She walked off again on the arm of the tall man in a jacket the color of a cardinal and the frightening hat of blackbird hue.

⁓⬙⬙⬙⁓

With nightingales it is easy.

The males secure their territory and launch into song. A female flutters to each of them at dawn and listens. They pour forth their souls, striving with every ounce of their beings to thrill the sleepy air (and her heart) into ecstasy.

Her decision is simple. She settles with the singer whose songs are filled with surprises and fancy sounds. Chirps, buzzes, warbles, trills, whistles.

It may be that an unusual string of notes persuades her she has found a father smart enough to provide food and protection during nesting time. Or it may simply be that she loves music that surprises her. The process takes one or two mornings at most.

When I was a year old, I returned to the tree where I was born. My mother was nowhere to be found that year, and I never did learn what became of her. But another female was hiding in the underbrush, hopping quietly about, and early one morning I chose a prominent perch high in the plum tree and poured out my heart to her.

And she accepted my song as her own. Our lives merged. The thrill of mating. The labor of nest-building and of gathering food for the young.

With the earthbound, it is not so simple.

What are the rules? What are the qualities that a female prizes in a male? How does she come to her decision?

There is more to the courtship than singing. But what that may be, I don't know. And humans don't seem to know either.

J

To be five feet tall and try to impress a proud woman with the beauty of your soul—well, it's not so easy. Especially when you are a cauldron of hot fire and cold doubts and, what's more, possess a strange penchant for solitude.

But *she* is different.

From the very first, we seem to know one another. The tide of our thoughts and desires floods us both equally.

I expect the course of our love to run smoothly. But almost as soon as she draws me in, I sense a change.

In love, as in poetry, I founder.

Fanny Brawne and her mother glide into the front parlor in the Dilkeses' half of Wentworth Place.

"So good to see you again, my friends!" Mrs. Dilkes exclaims, clearly cherishing the bonds they formed when the Brawnes rented half of Brown's house the summer he and I hiked the Lake District.

Taking in her light, erect posture; her quick, graceful motions; and her hyper-alert blue eyes, I confirm my first impression in Brown's garden: Fanny Brawne alters the world around her as the moon tugs the oceans across the face of the earth.

Already, I fear her power. Exhausted from several weeks of caring for Tom, I know I lack the strength to hold my own.

How can I even converse with such a creature? She flits about so airily that trying to capture a quiet moment with her would be like trying to hold a hummingbird in your hands. At times, she is monstrous in her behavior, flying out in all directions, calling people such names—not perhaps from any innate vice but from a penchant she has for acting stylishly.

"Where is Mr. Brown?" she demands, glancing toward his half of the house.

"Not in tonight," someone answers.

"Too bad," she replies. "His bald pate reflects the light so faithfully, it doubles the candlepower in the room. What about Haydon?"

"He is in his studio working on *Christ's Entry,*" the pleasant and matronly Mrs. Dilkes responds.

"Ah, yes, the painting that will liberate mankind from its poverty and ignorance." She glances toward me, and her blue eyes narrow. "Mr. Keats, I believe your face appears on his canvas, does it not?" she inquires.

I nod. "Haydon did me the favor of asking me to pose for his work."

"How nice. Did he ask you to pay for the favor?"

I feel the color rise in my face. "Certainly not."

"Not yet, anyway." She takes a few steps toward me and eyes me with cool detachment. "In the painting, your head is above Wordsworth's. I imagined you were taller." She shrugs and turns away.

Soon afterwards, I join her mother for a chat. She is a plump, confident woman, comfortable on her feet, with a shrewd light in her grey eyes.

"We understand you are devoting yourself at present to the care of your brother," she says with a look of sympathy.

I describe the past several weeks, how difficult they have been for Tom, what a brave fight he is putting up.

"How fortunate that you are trained in medicine."

I agree but add that I have ceased the practice of medicine to try my fortunes as a poet. A look of surprise flashes across her face, and the conversation ends soon thereafter.

I try to banter my way through the evening with various friends and acquaintances, but Tom is never far from my thoughts, and I end up by myself at a table, cracking and eating walnuts.

Sometime later, Fanny Brawne comes over and strikes a pose near me, and I hazard a smile, which she doesn't return. Her pale skin contrasts deliciously with her dark brown hair, which she's gathered in a fashionable mound on top of her head.

Her delicate eyebrows lift at the middle. "It's been no more than a few weeks since my family rented rooms over there." She nods toward Brown's half of the house. "Since your *friend* informed us we had to leave."

I can think of no tactful way to reply. I take the nutcracker in hand, place it about the shell of the walnut, and squeeze. The shell shatters, and pieces fly everywhere.

She gives a delighted laugh, kneels on the floor, and helps me retrieve the pieces from under the chairs and the sideboard. We seat ourselves at the table and start to pick out the meat. After a few minutes, she favors me with her gaze.

"I've been watching you tonight. Something is troubling you."

I try another smile. "I could never be gloomy in the presence of one so lively and unguarded as yourself."

She tilts her head. "You think me simple, then?"

I pause. "Hardly."

She frowns. "Just rude?"

"I don't mean to offend you," I tell her.

Her brilliant blue eyes peer directly into mine. "But you *are* gloomy tonight. You can't hide it."

I nod. "All right, yes. It's …" I try to tell her about Tom, but something strange is happening to me. Words are failing me.

She touches me lightly on the shoulder. "I'm sorry. I've upset you."

I shake my head.

"Then what is it?" she asks. Her voice is soft and gentle, a tone I don't expect from her, and it disarms me.

"It's my brother Tom," I say miserably. "I … we're losing him." Tears stream down my face.

Her eyes grow round as blueberries.

"I heard he was ill," she says. "I didn't know how ill." She pats my hand. "I'm very sorry, Mr. Keats."

"He's nearly gone," I tell her in a choking voice. "A few more days at most." She gets up, finds a handkerchief, and hands it to me.

"I believe he is most fortunate to have such a brother," she tells me. She seems about to say something else but chooses to remain silent. Finally, in a lighter voice, she volunteers, "A skilled practitioner has no need of a nutcracker, you know."

"No need of a nutcracker?" My voice is returning.

"Indeed not." Her delicate lashes give a soft flutter. "Might I show you?"

"Lead on, MacDuff," I reply.

She regards me archly. "That's Shakespeare. I'm not such an ignorant girl as you think. Now watch closely, sir." She places one walnut on the table and picks up a second nut, turning it so that the ridge—the overlap—is facing downward. "It's a simple matter of leverage."

Using both hands, she presses the top shell down upon the bottom shell. She gives a loud grunt.

Nothing happens.

"One more time," she says. This time she stands up and presses down with all her weight.

Again, nothing happens.

"This has *never* not worked," she contends.

"Some nuts are tougher than others," I suggest.

She juts out her lower lip and blows a strand of hair off her forehead. It is a young and unguarded gesture, and it contrasts with her fashionable clothes and hair in such a way that my heart pauses a moment, then starts racing.

"Mr. Keats, would you kindly press down upon my hands? I fear that it will take our combined strength to accomplish this."

I come up cautiously behind her. She is about my height— maybe half an inch taller. With tender diffidence, like someone approaching a sacred altar, I place my arms around her slender waist. She smells wonderful. Her hands are warm and exceedingly smooth. She shows no discomfort at our closeness. There is about her no false modesty.

From across the room, I sense Mrs. Brawne watching us.

"Ready … now!" Fanny exclaims. Her body grows taut and her arms thrust downward with surprising strength. I add my strength to hers.

Crack! The shell breaks open.

Fanny is breathing heavily and her voice has a new, husky undertone. "There, you see, Mr. Keats, I know of what I speak."

I retreat a step, unable to answer.

VII

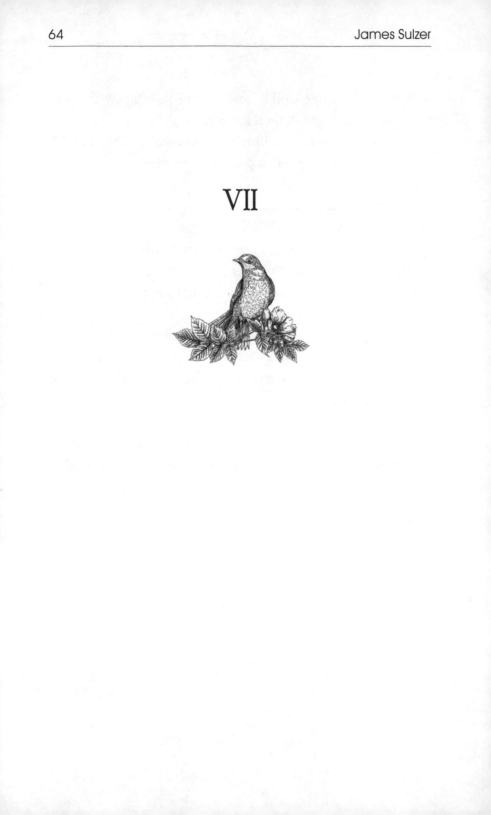

N

The three ruffians were back on their wheels, rushing toward the poet, who looked up with an expression of forbearance on his face.

You are on the road to ruin, Cockney poet.

Too bad. You are a boy of pretty abilities, which you've done everything in your power to spoil.

Next time, John, be a little more sparing of soporifics.

Once again, in perfect unison, they each raised a leg, but this time something strange intervened. At that moment, from I know not where, a fury entered my soul.

J

In utter silence, with no warning or indication of its newfound fervor, my little spirit companion shoots through the air toward my critics with tremendous speed and force, striking each in turn. They topple off their velocipedes, land on their backs, and release their streams of urine into the air directly above their prone bodies. The foul liquid splatters down like a rain shower upon their upturned faces.

Their eyes pulsate and their mouths turn inside out. It is a glorious sight.

They clamber back to their feet, climb onto their pathetic vehicles, and propel themselves off into obscurity.

In the wake of this declaration of friendship, I now have a loyal shadow. Like a cat that finally accepts you and deposits itself on your lap, this spirit is now a tireless petitioner of my attention. It hovers in the air before me, its gleam so radiant that it grows almost irksome. I am now able to detect the shifting outlines of its shape—an oval of indeterminate size.

Spirit, what do you wish of me? What are you trying to tell me?

Your buoyant companionship does little to change the truth: As a poet, and in all other ways, I was a failure.

N

I admit that the universe weighed in against the poet. But there is room still for hope. Surely his heartfelt apology to his sister soon afterwards must count in his favor.

The poet insists on calling his life a complete failure.

But how can that be? Hasn't he won my loyalty? Doesn't that also count for something?

I must find some way to tell him this.

I am beginning to feel the frustration that I cannot.

J

In the latter months of 1818, the heights and depths of my emotions are as dramatic as the mountains and chasms in the Lake District. Tom's rapid decline and my soaring affection for Fanny Brawne completely alter the landscape of my life.

My only source of comfort is William Shakespeare. When I feel like a failure in love, I console myself with his well-known lines on the subject. And when I grow anxious over the outcome of my romance with Fanny, I tell myself to emulate Shakespeare's greatest trait, which I call Negative Capability:

allowing oneself to dwell in a state of uncertainties, mysteries, and doubts.

These twin rudders help steady my soul as I navigate Tom's illness while also trying to advance my courtship of Fanny Brawne. But as Shakespeare reminds us, the course of true love never did run smooth.

Before our next meeting, I compose a card for Fanny, in which I declare myself her vassal.

Why wait? I am already hers.

From Brown's half of the house, it is no more than a few steps to the Dilkeses' parlor and its evening gatherings, its lit candles, its polished silver, its trays of sweets … and *her*.

While a few blocks away, my brother fights for his life.

N

In the stone house, Tom's eyes glared deep in their sockets. As evening gave way to the dreadful hours when owls frighten their prey from hiding, he was overcome by fits of coughing. He choked up streams of bright red blood, while the poet held a cloth to his mouth. By now, his brother was as pale as starlight, as thin as a shadow.

Finally, toward morning, Tom's breath found a new rhythm, quieter and easier, and he settled onto one side. He snuggled his head into the pillow and set his lips. Then the breathing slowed and came to a stop. The poet buried his face in his hands. "Dear Tom," he cried, "you are finally free." His body shook like an ash tree in a storm.

Three young people stood beside an open grave, hugging each other and sobbing. Off to the side lurked Raven man, his face blank behind his flashing spectacles. He nodded to a man dressed in black, who tossed the first clod of dirt into the grave. It landed with an empty thud, like the sound a wounded bird makes when it strikes the ground.

Soon we were lifted to the Dilkeses' parlor. A small crowd had gathered for a party. Talking and laughing. A table on the side overflowed with drinks and food.

J

The card rests in the inner pocket of my vest as I pass through the door that separates the two halves of Wentworth Place—Brown's side, where I now rent a room, and the Dilkeses'.

Fanny is already there, engaged in spirited conversation with Mrs. Dilkes and her mother. She is dressed in grey, and her hair is piled neatly on top of her head, tied with a dark blue ribbon that accents her eyes. I stand nearby and wait, my heart fluttering like a robin feeding on hawthorne berries.

She takes no notice of me.

I'm still waiting when Haydon saunters into the room, smoothing his vest over his round belly. The painter's gloomy face brightens when he sees me, and he bumbles over, an intent look in his eyes. He rests a hand on my shoulder and—without even mentioning Tom—he unleashes a long speech upon me. His life has hit some snags. Because of difficulties with his eyesight, he has suspended his work on *Christ's Entry*. After several minutes of this, he pauses, asks me how I am, and finally expresses sympathy for the loss of Tom. Then, in a tone of voice meant to sound casual, he inquires if the estate has been settled.

"Not yet," I reply, recoiling a bit at his directness. "I antici-
pate that a portion of Tom's share should come my way at some
point."

"I assume it will be of substance?" Haydon asks with a
quick touch of the tip of his tongue to his lips (one of his less
attractive habits).

"I hope it will be enough to allow me to work and study for
a good while. But, of course, that remains to be seen."

"Of course." Haydon steps closer, dips his head in an ingra-
tiating way, and reveals more about his present difficulties. He
needs money to stage an exhibit for two of his art students. He
needs funds to cure his eyesight so that he can move forward
on his masterpiece. He is quite far in arrears and needs cash
for rent and for food. In short, he has fallen on hard times and
knows no one else so generous.

"Is there any chance you can be of assistance to a friend
who has advanced your career and always held you in high regard?" he asks.

It seems cruel to say no to a friend in need. I am confident
that something will come my way from the estate. But the tim-
ing and the amount are in doubt.

I place my hand on Haydon's shoulder. "As soon as the
money is released, I will let you know." It is meant as a plea for
more time, but he disregards that subtlety. He bows, calls me a
great man, and strolls off across the room with a new swagger.
He secures a drink and inserts himself with brio into the conversation between Fanny, her mother, and Mrs. Dilkes.

Charles Brown is beside me. "Was Haydon trying to pry
some money from you?"

I confirm that he was.

"The worm. He tried earlier with me. I told him to bug off."
He shambles away, shaking his head.

The party is entering its final hour when Fanny pulls herself away from her mother and flows across the room, waving a fuchsia-colored fan next to her face.

She spots me and catches my eye. "I am sorry for your loss, Mr. Keats."

I reach forward, thinking she is about to offer her hand, but she stops several feet short of me. "We all feel sympathy for this unfortunate event," she adds.

Her blue eyes, normally so piercingly clear, are foggy and seem to be edging off to the side.

She pivots and exits the room, leaving a chill behind.

I accept her mother's invitation to join her and Mrs. Dilkes, but once the two matrons have offered their deepest sympathy for my loss, the conversation falters, darting here and there like the flight of a wayward swallow. Eventually, we stumble upon the subject of my plans for the future, and I sense Mrs. Brawne watching me closely. I mention that I expect to be going to London soon to settle Tom's estate, which I admit (knowing full well the power of such a statement) shows every promise of being quite substantial. The two women exchange a glance.

At the end of the evening, I return to my room and pull up a chair by the fire. Fumbling Fanny's card out of my vest pocket, I feast my eyes upon it one last time.

Then, with the strange sense of release that comes of such acts, I lean forward and feed it to the flames. The card catches, blooms in a yellow and red blossom, and crumbles into a pile of ash.

N

As the poet brooded by the fire, there was a knock on the door, and Charles Brown entered, handing him an envelope—a card of a different sort, printed in shiny black letters. The poet looked at it once, then again, shook his head, and read it over a third time.

A small cottage, surrounded by leafless trees and a shivering rose bush. Smoke rising from a chimney. Through the windows, the silhouettes of humans chopping vegetables, stacking wood, washing. A green wreath tied onto the front door with a red ribbon.

J

"Merry Christmas," I cry, and the door flies open.

"It's John Keats—rosy cheeks and all!" Fanny flows up beside me, pats me on the cheek, and asks for my coat. I look around the room and try to sort what I see.

The Brawnes are a tangle of activity. Besides Fanny, who is eighteen, there is Samuel, fourteen, and little Margaret, only eleven. There is no father; they lost Mr. Brawne eight years earlier from consumption, and Mrs. Brawne watches over the brood with shrewd attentiveness.

But it is Fanny who rules them.

She is everywhere—hanging my coat on a peg, ordering Margaret to clean up the clay she's been playing with, snapping at Samuel to bring in more fuel from the woodpile—even advising her mother about the dishes she's cooking. "The stew needs more pepper, Mother," she pronounces, stationing herself by the stove. She crosses her ankles, dips a large spoon into the pot, and sips elegantly from one side. "And don't you think a bit of thyme would help?" She clatters the top back down.

"I find I am always in need of more time," I put in.

"No more of that from you, sir!" Fanny wags a finger at me.

Mrs. Brawne gives me a look: *Do you see what I have to deal with?* She lifts the top of the pot and adds pepper and thyme to the stew.

The activity in the home never slows its frenetic pace. Samuel, hammer and saw in hand, is constructing some sort of slingshot. Margaret is drawing a portrait of a dog and is simultaneously whining that she wants a puppy. The children grow restless as they wait for dinner, and I invite them to join me in a game some friends and I have devised. It's quite simple: Each person takes the part of an orchestral instrument, and through the ingenuity of the human voice and various whistles and other appropriate (and inappropriate) sounds, we create a concert.

My instrument has always been the loudest and most comical of them all, the bassoon. Samuel chooses to be the percussion section, with clashing cymbals and pattering drums, while Margaret takes the part of the screechy violin. And Fanny, when she cares to join us in her travels to and fro across the room, adds an airy flute, wiggling her fingers daintily.

We devise our melody as we go, a raucous and rambunctious descent into pure anarchy, and for several minutes our cacophony fills the room. Somewhere deep inside me, I feel a flicker of light and warmth returning. The music lurches through a massive crescendo to its joyful conclusion, horribly and wonderfully out of tune.

After dinner, Fanny and I are left on the sofa by the fire while the others retire for a nap.

"I hope my family has not alarmed you," she offers, sipping at a cup of tea.

"Your family is wonderful."

She places her cup down on the side table.

"I was rude to you a few weeks ago," she says. "I was distant and unsympathetic."

"You were." I turn toward her. Her eyes are ardent and clear.

"If it helps at all, it was not really my doing," she explains. "My mother had told me I was being too forward with you." Her mouth twists. "She said I was throwing myself at you."

"I never felt that." I lift my hand, pause, and place it on hers.

She allows my hand to remain there. "She warned me against you and told me to keep my distance—which is why I was so dreadful to you on that night. I hated myself for it."

"I was puzzled by it."

She squeezes my hand. "Then later that same evening, Mother said she'd been talking to Mrs. Dilkes, and for some reason she'd changed her mind about you. She said it would be all right to invite you over for Christmas if I wanted that—which, of course, I did."

"Thank God for the Dilkeses."

"I have no idea *why* she changed her mind. But I do know that my mother fears for my future. It hasn't been easy for her—losing Father, having to raise the three of us on her own. She thinks I should be set up for life with a man of wealth." Her lip curls, just slightly.

"Not a bad wish, certainly," I observe.

Her eyes flash. "And what do you mean by that?" She draws her hand away.

I reach over and take her hand, gazing deep into her eyes and feeding on her rich anger. "I meant nothing, except to say that your mother was only thinking of your welfare."

Her eyes waver. "Mr. Keats, are you trifling with me?" she asks.

"That would be impossible. If anything, I am doing the very opposite of that." I try to catch her eye.

"Are you sure?" Her eyebrows arch upwards in the nicest way.

"I am more than sure." I heave a sigh. "But I do wish that I were wealthy. For if I were, all that I have would be yours."

"I don't care if you're wealthy," she whispers, in a low and thrilling voice. She leans in close to me and touches her face against mine.

"You don't?"

She moans or laughs softly, the nicest sound I've ever heard. Our heads turn, and for the first time, gently and lightly, we kiss. "I don't care one bit about those things. It's you I care about," she whispers into my ear.

The hair on the back of my neck is rising. We kiss again. And again.

I've never felt such ecstasy. Her lips, her tongue, the delicious warm fragrance of her skin.

We part only when Margaret steps into the room and lets out a scream.

ℕ

How could I not rejoice at this turn of events? The poet loved deeply and was loved in return. Their love was in balance.

J

Our love is out of balance.

When we are together, it is as close to ecstasy as we mortals are granted. But each time we part, I feel torn in two. The pleasure of her kisses is so delicious, the tone of her voice so lovely, the radiance of her beauty so stunning, I can hardly bear the agony of separation.

Then, after being away from her a few days, I notice an odd change—like the partial healing of a wound, or the icing over of a lake. I am still dazzled by her. I am still at her mercy. But as I start to separate from her, I begin to shy away. I fear her power over me.

It is the fear that by loving her too much, I will lose her. It is also the fear of being engulfed, of losing myself in the vastness of this newly awakened need.

Then there is a practical issue. In order to write, I need time and solitude.

N

A rock wall in the silver shadows of a winter afternoon.

J

An expression too quick to read flashes across Fanny's face. "But, John, why must you go away?"

I take her hand and try to explain. The importance of solitude when I am writing. My great hopes for my literary endeavors. How hard it has been to come to this decision.

Her pupils contract into two points. "But aren't you alone all day in your half of Wentworth Place, with no one but Brown for company?"

"I care for you too much," I tell her. "I am in danger of losing myself in the epic expanse of my affection."

She shakes her head. "That makes no sense."

"I've told myself the same thing," I reply miserably. "But I know this is something I must do."

I pull her close and kiss her. She returns my kisses with delicate little flutters of her tongue that torture me with unfulfilled desire. Her eyes regard me now from a distance.

And so I leave for the seaside town of Chichester—to live and write—alone.

VIII

N

The fury that choked my heart when the men with wheels mistreated the poet came back—but this time I felt it toward the poet himself. It was the same feeling that came over me when one of my fledglings took off on a sudden flight into an area where a hawk was hunting.

I darted back and forth in front of the poet.

He gave me a surprised look. "Spirit? What are you doing?" He waved an arm at me.

I fluttered closer and began to chastise him for his stupidity. Why had he left his soul mate? What reason was there to destroy the very best that his life had to offer? What was he thinking?

But, of course, I had no voice and wasn't heard.

J

I am under attack from this volatile spirit, and for no apparent reason. The little pest lunges closer, hovering inches from my face, like a bumblebee trying to drive someone from its home. I wave my hand the way you might try to brush off a fly or a mosquito. It is meant only in warning—and I am shocked to feel the impact when I strike the little spirit, smite it quite hard with the back of my hand, and send it hurtling headlong into the night.

N

With the force of his savage blow I found myself tumbling toward the earth—dazed and confused and unable to stop my fall despite turning this way and that and opening my wings for support.

As I sailed closer to the earth, the poet and pugilist's moody adventures in love seemed to have advanced by a leap of six weeks.

J

Our eyes meet from opposite sides of the Dilkeses' parlor, and she takes one step in my direction but stops. "This is a surprise. To what do we owe the pleasure?"

"Brown sent me word about the Valentine's Day party here." I hazard a smile, which she doesn't return.

"I see."

"I wanted to surprise you."

"You did."

"It's been six weeks now since I left for Chichester."

"I know." She sniffs slightly. "I trust you've been well."

"Very well," I reply.

"I am so happy to hear that." She turns away.

Haydon appears at my elbow and inquires about my writing. "There's not much to speak of," I tell him gloomily, watching Fanny greet an admirer. She is resplendent in a dazzling red gown edged with blue trim. "How are you?"

"Oh, the same as ever. It's been a tedious winter." After a bit more small talk, he asks if I have been to see Mr. Abbey.

"Mr. Abbey?" I ask.

A muscle in his jaw twitches. "To settle your brother's share of the estate."

"Oh, that." I shake my head. "Alas, no. News about the estate has been slow to develop."

"I'm sorry to hear that." His tongue touches his lips. "But perhaps you can spare a few quid for a friend?"

I sigh and look up toward the ceiling, unsure how to respond. But at that moment, a deus ex machina arrives in the person of Charles Brown. He presses himself between Haydon and me, jostling Haydon hard enough to slosh most of his glass of wine onto his vest.

"What the devil!" Haydon exclaims, patting his chest. "What's wrong with you, Brown?"

"There's nothing wrong with me. It's you that's in the wrong," Brown growls.

Haydon brushes the last of the liquid off his vest with the attentive air of someone grooming a pureblood dog. "Whatever are you talking about?"

"I'm telling you to leave Keats alone. He needs every last bit of money that he has."

Haydon's face condenses into a snarl. "And I'm telling you to mind your own business, Charles Brown."

"This *is* my business! I need his damn rent money." Brown looks as if he would like to punctuate his comments to Haydon with another shove, but a cry from across the room stops him short.

"There he is, the rogue!" A female voice shrieks so loudly that the party falls quiet. Guests peer about the room to see what could possibly be the matter.

Brown spins on his heels, straightens the collar of his evening jacket, and strides toward Fanny. As always, he is rock solid on his thick, muscular legs. His shaven head gleams in the candlelight, and he cracks a ragged smile. "Dear lady, are you referring to me, perchance?"

Over Christmas, Brown remarked more than once on how much time I was spending with Fanny, and he confided that he sometimes felt snubbed by her when they met on the street. But he never revealed to me his decision to retaliate against her.

He and Fanny stand a few feet apart, regarding each other with a strange brew of dislike and attraction. "You found my valentine verse to your liking, I trust?" he asks in a loud and theatrical voice.

"It was scandalous," she replies, wrinkling her nose. The twisting of her features, ironically, only emphasizes their beauty.

His ragged smile grows broader. "As it should be ... for I was writing about a scandalous young woman."

The energy of their exchange perplexes me.

Fanny places one foot before the other, arches her right arm dramatically, and recites the verse from memory. When she is finished, she shakes the valentine at Brown and demands, "How dare you suggest that I should have been whipped at school for being naughty!"

Brown gives a sweeping bow. "It was the very least you deserved. My deep sense of propriety—as well my sensitivity for the feelings of the fairer sex—prevented me from suggesting even harsher punishments."

"You should be ashamed of yourself, saying such things to a respectable woman."

"And so I would—if I were speaking to a respectable woman. Which, my lady, you ain't."

She shakes the valentine again. "You heed my words, Charles Brown. Henceforth, for the remainder of your life—however long or short that may be—you shall live in fear of my response."

"On the contrary, my lady, I shall eagerly await it," Brown answers. "As of this evening, my life is finally complete, and I am content."

Fanny throws back her head. "Well, I am not content, sir, not at all, now that my reputation has been toyed with in such an indecorous manner."

Their voices rumble on. Unnoticed, I slip out of the room, my heart tumbling.

N

And I still tumbled through the air like a baby sparrow shoved out of its nest by a cuckoo. How far would I fall? The blue earth streamed toward me.

A great city took shape beneath me—buildings, roads, fountains. I braced myself for the impact that must surely be coming, anticipating that it would be more painful than the blow I'd already received.

But then a pair of large hands reached out and gathered me in.

J

For a novice, I find I can fly at will and zip about with rather good control, and I manage to overtake the little spirit and capture it in my cupped hands.

By now its shape is coming into more focus, and I can make out its small birdlike head, which swivels on its neck and peers up at me.

"I'm very sorry, little spirit, I wasn't trying to strike you. Really, I wasn't. I hope you aren't hurt."

The spirit opens its mouth as if to reply, but nary a peep comes out.

N

It was just as well that the poet couldn't hear me, for I was making good use of every human swear word I'd learned so far. And they weren't the polite versions a proper little dove might use, like *Duck you* or *Flock you*.

J

The little spirit flutters out of my hands and hovers at a distance from me. We are almost as close to the earth now as we were at our first meeting—I can espy the grey procession of the Spanish Steps and the distant dark hollow of the Colosseum—and we resume our slow, upward drift while, below us, my life continues to unfold in excruciating detail.

※⟨♡⟩⟫

It is springtime. Several weeks have passed since the Valentine's Day fiasco. When the carriage pulls up, I am outside, retrieving a kitchen chair from under the plum tree.

I look up, a taste of ashes in my mouth. I know all about the new tenants—the result of the Dilkeses' decision that spring to move to London and rent out their half of Wentworth Place to the Brawnes.

The carriage rumbles to a halt and she steps out, wearing a short-sleeved summer dress with prints of Grecian maidens with lyres and flutes. I observe her in stunned silence. Everything about her is exquisite—her face, her figure, and most of all, her alert and ardent presence in the world.

As winter gave way to spring, we kept our distance from each other. Now, like Pyramus and Thisbe, we will be separated by a single wall.

She retrieves her bag and takes a few emphatic but graceful steps toward the house. Her plaited hair swings lightly beside her long, intelligent face.

What can I do except stride over? "May I take that for you, young lady?"

She stops and trains her pale blue eyes on me.

"Oh, yes, thank you." She sets down the bag. "Do I know you, sir?"

I pick up the bag and walk ahead of her. My face is starting to burn.

"I'm sure I've seen you before, but truly, it's been so long—weeks, months, in fact—that I believe I've forgotten your name," she continues.

I carry on in silence.

"Let's see … is it David? Or Leigh? Or Benjamin? Oh, I know. It's Charles! Yes! It's Charles, isn't it?"

We arrive at the entrance to the Brawnes' half of the house.

"Hmm … could that be wrong? I thought I heard there was a Charles who lived here," she muses.

Once we are inside, I glance back at her for directions, and she nods. "Anywhere will be fine."

I set down the bag.

"Well, then, I'll be going now." I give her a quick look and try to push past her.

She thrusts out her arm. "John, wait!" she exclaims in a new, more urgent tone. "We need to talk."

I stop and turn toward her.

She draws in a quick breath. "Are those tears in your eyes?"

"What did you expect?" I ask.

"What do you mean?" Her eyes grow wide.

"For treating me so horridly," I blurt out.

She places her hand on my forearm, and her fingers slide gently back and forth across my wrist.

"John, please listen. I believe it was *you* who treated *me* horridly. Leaving me for weeks … saying you needed to be away from me."

She gives a look both accusing and beseeching.

"All right, so I go away for a while to write, and then finally, I come back." I gaze past her, up toward the ceiling. "And on that day you receive a valentine from someone else—and then you crow about it from the rooftops for everybody to hear. All the while laughing secretly at me."

She shakes her head. "I was having fun with the valentine … to see if you would rise to the bait. But instead you disappeared."

I lower my gaze. "Well, what did you expect?"

She pauses a moment. "I'm sorry, I'm so sorry. I only meant it as a joke."

"You meant it as a joke?"

"Of course. Brown is an old man … well, almost. And anyway, he's not the one I care for."

I consider all this in silence. I feel, astonishingly, that I may be about to shed weeks of distress in one mad rush, like a mass of snow sliding off a roof.

Her face is very near. Her eyes are tender.

"Do you realize how much I missed you?" she asks. It is her quiet voice, the voice I love.

"Oh, God, I've missed you so much, Fanny," I confess.

Our faces incline toward each other.

"We are both too stubborn for our own good, my darling boy," she whispers. We kiss once, and again.

There is a shriek. Margaret has stepped inside.

"Smooching again!" she yowls. "Don't you two ever stop?"

N

We had drifted as high above the earth as the canopy of my plum tree.

Now that I had experienced a taste of fury and frustration, I was more concerned than ever about the poet's state, after the massive heartstorms he'd endured in his life.

Thankfully, with Fanny Brawne, he had finally found a happy ending.

But between the poet and myself, all was not happy. He had struck me, and struck me hard. Even if it was by chance, I refused to venture close to him anytime soon.

After a bit, he called over to me through the gloom. "Spirit? May we have a talk?"

What now?

"I know you're angry at me, but please—"

I pulsed a few times. Oh, all right.

J

The spirit pulses like a firefly and floats closer, while maintaining some separation to indicate its displeasure.

For which I blame it not one bit. At the very least, I have wounded its humble pride.

I too have pride. The pride that sustained me during my lifetime—much of it anyway—was vain and boastful. There's no need for that strain of pride any longer.

Instead, there's the need for candor, to pour out my heart to the spirit, laying out the details of my many failings. How I was divided against myself for much of my life—trapped by a lack of belief in myself, by oversensitive nerves, by tempestuous emotions—and how, for a time, I had to rely on a drug to dull my senses. How, also for a time, I satisfied the needs of my flesh through visits to women who were desperate enough to give themselves for money. Looking back at my life, I confide to the spirit, I marvel that anyone was able to put up with me—and most of all, that Fanny Brawne accepted me into her heart. Which she did. For a time.

But only for a time, I confess.

$\mathcal{N}$

So much for the happy ending.

IX

J

By fits and starts, my tender spirit and I are growing better acquainted. But there is something still buried—my secret plunge into the rotten fumes of the river Styx.

Did you know what finally freed me to find my voice as a poet?

The spirit pulses like a firefly, and a very loud one.

N

Something more than his struggles to be a poet? The Immortal Dinner? The hike through the Lake District? Speaking his verse for William Wordsworth?

J

I continue: *I know we relived the Immortal Dinner, so of course you know something. There were so many twists and turns along the way, they dizzy the memory. And then the deep descents into self-doubt I would rather forget.*

The spirit pulses.

Can you help me find my way through this way station and move on to … to whatever comes next?

Again the spirit pulses—though I'm not sure what it means.

Could you serve as my guide through the process that determines the final sum of my life? Which I fear will summon a return of that monstrous balance scale?

More pulsing.

So be it. Will you conjure up two memories from the depths of my torpor in the winter and spring of 1819?

The spirit pulses in a steady rhythm that seems to signify *I will try.*

⁂

I'm seated at my desk, fumbling through some papers, looking sluggish and a bit dazed. It's early spring, a month after the Valentine's Day wounds, still a month before the Brawnes will move next door. Fanny and I are securely estranged from each other.

In the next yard the oak tree is bare, having lost the last of the leaves that hung on all winter. As yet, there's no new growth.

It's a period in my life when I keep largely to myself, trying to write, with little success. Each day, my heart sends out more condemnation and pain than the one before.

After several minutes of aimless paper shuffling, I stand up, wander over to my dresser, and pick up a small bottle. Screwing open the top, I pour a thick amber liquid into a spoon, raise it to my mouth, and swallow it, grimacing at its bitterness but licking every last bit off the spoon.

It is laudanum.

Beside me, the spirit is pulsing, as if alarmed by what it sees.

There was a fight, I tell the spirit. *A joust—a second joust, to be more precise—over a kitten this time instead of my little brother. This pernicious bottle was the unfortunate result.*

The spirit pulses.

N

Dried-up brown leaves clung to the lower branches of the oak trees: a cold day, midwinter. Out on a walk, the poet happened upon a boy in an apron bent over a gutter, holding a struggling mass in his arms. Creeping closer to investigate this odd sight, the poet discovered that the boy had trapped a kitten between his arms and was slapping it time and again with the flat side of a knife. The creature's weak, pathetic cries were horrible to hear for the human poet, though I might have felt differently.

The poet hurried up to the boy, swore at him to stop this nonsense, and gave him a shove. The knife flew off and clattered into the street, and taking advantage of the confusion, the kitten dashed off to the safety of a tree.

The boy scrambled to his feet and turned toward my poet. Though he looked younger, he was taller and broader in the shoulders.

"You think you can whip me, do you?" he asked. "You, little man?"

The poet circled in toward him, fists raised. The boy swung and missed. The poet pounced on the boy and wrestled him down. They rolled about in the gritty street and exchanged a few glancing blows.

"Here, you ... stop it!" a voice bellowed. A massive creature grabbed the poet by the collar and yanked him away. "What're you doin' to my lit'l brother?"

Struggling for breath, the poet stood and faced the giant. When he saw who it was, he gave a start. The giant wore an apron covered with animal parts and smears of blood. He looked the poet up and down, and his broad face shifted like a slab of sliding ice.

"Why, it's you, ain't it, you lit'l shit!" he exclaimed. He rolled up a sleeve and took a step toward the poet. "I been waitin' for this moment for years, I 'ave."

The poet slammed into the giant and started to pummel his stomach. The giant brushed the poet away, drew back, and landed a bone-crunching punch on his face. The poet lurched back, fell onto one knee, regrouped, and took a fighting stance again a few feet in front of the giant.

J

The world is spinning about me like a carousel, and I know I'm in grave danger, but I can't think clearly enough to imagine an escape.

"You get back in 'ere!" a voice yells. Through the fog of my vision, I discern a woman looming large in the doorway of a shop, arms crossed. "You get in 'ere and finish up your work or you'll be sorry. And leave that lit'l boy alone."

The butcher wipes his hands on his apron and spits contemptuously onto the street. "You're a lucky one, you are," he snarls. "Now begone with you, and don't come back 'ere again. Or you'll be sorry."

I raise myself to my full height, give a stiff bow, and stumble away. I am distantly aware of how ludicrous it is that I'm trying to maintain my dignity at such a moment. With each step, my head throbs as though it's been struck by a hammer.

Brown jumps to his feet as I stagger into the parlor. "My God, what happened to you?"

Though it's only a day later, I've already set aside my annoyance at Brown about the valentine; my real quarrel is with Fanny Brawne. I wave a hand toward my friend.

"It's nothing."

Brown arrests my motion with a hand. "Nothing? You're a bloody mess! Better let me take a look."

"I got in a fight with a butcher's boy who was tormenting a cat." I collapse with a thud onto a chair and wince. "I administered quite a beating, but the big brother came and things took a turn for the worse."

Brown bends down, peers at my face, and tsks. "Good thing it's winter—we can put ice on it. Does it hurt?"

"Perhaps a little."

"More than a little, I'll warrant." Brown purses his lips. "I have something you can use for the pain. Laudanum. It's very effective, but it has its dangers. Don't take too much at a time, and don't you dare ask for any more than what I give you." He goes outside and returns with a hunk of ice wrapped in a towel, then he clomps into the pantry to retrieve the laudanum.

Holding the ice to my eye, I accept the vial of liquid from Brown. A few minutes later I limp up to my bedroom, wondering what, if anything, the medicine can do.

Little spirit, there's no reason you would know anything about laudanum. It's a tincture—a liquid—used for a variety of ailments, mostly for pain. The most widely available version is about 10 percent opium and also contains morphine and codeine; it induces sleep and is said to cause visions. I'm guessing you've never heard of the poet Samuel Taylor Coleridge, but he claims that his poem "Kubla Khan" appeared to him complete, in a dream-vision, after a dose of laudanum.

The morning after my first dose, I can already feel its effects. I write in a letter to my brother George that I'm "in a sort of temper indolent and supremely careless." Of course, I don't admit to the use of laudanum. I mention my black eye to George, but claim it was caused by a ball striking my face during a game of cricket. George and Georgina are thousands of miles away now, in the Kentucky wilderness; there's no need to trouble them with news of the fight with our one-time usher.

Laudanum engulfs your senses like a cartful of the most fragrant lilacs. It induces a waking dream so seductive, I sometimes feel myself floating right out through the window and into the treetops.

After a month the vial runs out, and it's fortunate that I don't dare ask Brown for more. That prevents any serious addiction. For a few days afterward I feel restless and irritable, but I force myself to shake off the effects and even make an effort to start writing again.

But I'm unable to summon up the energy to start pushing that boulder up the hill.

Something is stopping me, and several weeks pass before I begin to understand what it is.

A kind of black cloud has gathered over and around me—like melancholy but thicker and more encompassing. Though I can't really understand it, I suspect that my spirits have been weighed down by the accumulation of tragedies in my life. All the deaths: my parents' death, my grandmother's death, the loss of Tom. And on top of that, the ups and downs of my love affair with Fanny Brawne.

What can be the point of a life of such heartache?

I know I'll be unable to write anything of value until I reach a better understanding of the pain and suffering that are everywhere in our world—in myself and also in others. What can be their purpose? Is there a purpose? I start to question the validity of this world—this place where parents die in their youth, where a brother fades into a spectre of himself and slips away decades too soon. I am in need of an abiding faith—perhaps something more definite, a philosophic framework—something to explain the mysterious dynamic that exists between the world, the self, and what we call the soul.

In recent years, my understanding of the world's vastness has changed. It expanded with my hike to the Lake District, where I encountered such a startling range of landscapes—jagged cliffs, gentle pastures, pellucid lakes. In a world with such variety, I conclude, an untroubled life is impossible. Just as the natural world contains hot deserts and cold poles, so our human lives must encounter extremes of all sorts.

No one is immune to the diverse challenges thrown before us. Life must be undergone.

In a letter to my brother George and his wife Georgina, so far away in Kentucky, I sort out these thoughts.

> The common cognomen of this world among the misguided and superstitious is 'a vale of tears,' from which we are to be redeemed by a certain arbitrary interposition of God and taken to Heaven—What a little circumscribed straightened notion! Call the world if you Please

'The vale of Soul-making.' Then you will find out the use of the world.

I say '*Soul making*'—Soul as distinguished from an Intelligence. There may be intelligences or sparks of the divinity in millions—but they are not Souls till they acquire identities, till each one is personally itself. Intelligences are atoms of perception—they know and they see and they are pure, in short they are God—how then are Souls to be made? How then are these sparks which are God to have identity given them—so as ever to possess a bliss peculiar to each one's individual existence? How, but by the medium of a world like this?

This is effected by three grand materials acting the one upon the other for a series of years—These three Materials are the *Intelligence*—the *human heart* (as distinguished from intelligence or Mind) and the *World* or *Elemental space* suited for the proper action of *Mind* and *Heart* on each other for the purpose of forming the *Soul* or *Intelligence destined to possess the sense of Identity.*

I will put it in the most homely form possible. I will call the *world* a School instituted for the purpose of teaching little children to read—I will call the *human heart* the *horn Book* used in that School—and I will call the *Child able to read*, the *Soul* made from that *school* and its *horn book*. Do you not see how necessary a World of Pains and troubles is to school an Intelligence and make it a Soul? A Place where the heart must feel and suffer in a thousand diverse ways.

As various as the Lives of Men are—so various become their Souls, and thus does God make individual beings, Souls, of the sparks of his own essence.

Once the letter is posted, I feel unburdened. I am ready to return to my poetry.

ℕ

The poet at his desk, filling up white squares of paper.

J

Kind spirit, can you endure a bit more information about my scribblings? For the odes that spring, I splice together two classic forms. I fashion a stanza of ten lines that marries two poetic traditions: the Shakespearean quatrain (ABAB) followed by the Petrarchian sestet (CDECDE). The merger happens more or less of itself as I set off down winding mossy ways toward a poetry all my own.

Each ode begins with a song of praise to an ideal symbol (for instance, a Grecian urn) counterpoised against our world of time and decay. Yet, it is also a world that is sensuous and rich beyond anything a chaste symbol can contain. Symbol and reality: Life is a compound of opposites. In the collision of cool symbol and warm world, I seek to render the complex harmonies of a poetic song never before heard.

N

I struggled to understand. These words were too dense with greenery to admit much light. But the way he stood straight and held his head high and spoke in a calm, clear voice—like a cardinal giving praise to an autumn morning—showed how strongly he believed what he said. The beauty he found and set in his verse was precious to him—like those bits of nature where I drew inspiration for my songs: a patch of blue on a still pond, a sliver of moon clenched like a talon in the afternoon sky, the thrum of my mate's wings when she returned to our nest.

⁕⁕〜⦅⚜⦆〜⁕⁕

It was a lovely, clear morning in late April, still quite early. The poet carried a chair from the breakfast table around to the front of the house. He set it on a patch of grass under my plum tree, seated himself, and brought out his white squares and his writing utensils. He leaned back, closed his eyes, and listened.

Above him, perched high in the tree, I sang. Out of the many bits and pieces in my heart, I wove a song of ecstasy.

J

I drink in the song of the bird and chase its joy with draughts of the sorrow I've known so intimately. Ecstasy and despair meet in a shock of opposites that transforms them both, and

I feel myself enter a strange state, a place of gentle repose. In this twilight world, the song of the nightingale is reborn as a strand in the eternal tapestry of light and darkness, weaving the weft of its eternal affirmation through the warp of time and change, of loss and longing. The nightingale and I are separate, yet joined forever.

𝒩

Finally, I understand what happened.

I was captured in a poem, liberated in a poem, transformed in a poem. A bird no more, I was now a spirit.

I have witnessed the moment the miracle took place, when I was ushered into the realm of words and poetry and became a spirit being.

My body has disappeared, but I remain.

And since that moment, through hearing the words of this poem and others, my education has lurched forward.

I was that bird, that light-winged dryad, but now I am something different, new. I understand the poet's words, reborn.

X

J

Later that afternoon, Fanny Brawne and her family arrive at Wentworth Place and settle in their half of the house. Over the next two weeks, with Fanny just a wall away, I write three more odes, one inspired by an urn on display at the British Museum, one suggested by a cloud of mist that shrouds Hampstead's green hills, and one influenced by a dream of a procession of shadowy figures. No matter its wellspring, each poem celebrates Fanny's return. The quest for love that can endure in the midst of decay. The intimate knowledge that binds deep joy and sadness. The difference between love that is real and the phantoms that impersonate love, ambition, poetry.

"What is it you're trying to say about these lovers on the vase?" she asks one afternoon. We are lounging side by side under the plum tree, and she has just read through "Ode on a Grecian Urn."

"Well, you might say the figures on the urn are fortunate, in a way—they will never grow old, never fade. They will never lose their love."

She strokes my arm. "But they'll never consummate their love on that bloody old vase. Is that a good thing?"

I let out a groan. "Definitely not. But at least they won't have …" I take the sheet of paper from her and read, "'a heart high-sorrowful and cloyed, a burning forehead, and a parching tongue.'"

"Oh, tsk," she says. "Is love really so bad in our world?"

I don't answer. Lying down, I rest my head in her lap, and with a gentle, unhurried air, she shreds a dandelion and scatters the pieces over me.

"I have another question for you, my Pyramus."

"Yes, Thisbe?"

She picks up another sheet from the poem and squints in the sunlight. "Do you really believe that 'Beauty is truth, truth beauty' is 'all ye need to know'? Really, John, isn't that rather simple?"

I stretch out my arm and stroke her cheek. "It's not I who's saying that, my dear."

"If not you, then who?" she asks, tickling my ear with the dandelion stem.

"It's the urn," I inform her.

"A talking urn. How shocking," she replies. "I hope it doesn't start walking about as well and demanding to be filled up with olive oil or wine."

I prop myself on my elbows. "You see, that sentence about beauty and truth—it's the message that the urn offers to us poor humans."

She frowns. "That beauty is truth?"

"Yes, well, that the beauty of this *moment* is true now, and therefore true forever." I take her hand and kiss it. "As we are reminded when we see it fixed for all time on the urn."

Her dark pupils contract. "But it's not *real* on the urn."

"Within its own world it is, I imagine."

She brings my hand to her lips. "Still, those figures on the urn must miss this, don't you think?" She leans down and touches her lips to mine.

I moan in pleasure and ask for another kiss.

A few minutes later, she pats her hand on the soft grass. "Now, my sweet poet, I demand to hear another of your creations."

I sit up and rummage through my books and papers. "Let's see. I have my 'Ode on Melancholy.' There's a part I wrote partly for you. To be perfectly candid, it *is* you."

"I don't see how it could be about me if there's *melancholy* involved," she replies.

"Well, as you may recall, I did experience some melancholy this winter."

"All your own doing," she tells me, tickling my throat with the dandelion stem.

"True enough." I shuffle through the papers. "Ah, yes, here's the passage."

I clear my throat and read.

> But when the melancholy fit shall fall
>   Sudden from heaven like a weeping cloud,
> That fosters the droop-headed flowers all,
>   And hides the green hill in an April shroud;
> Then glut thy sorrow on a morning rose,
>   Or on the rainbow of the salt-sand wave,
>   Or on the wealth of globed peonies;
> Or if thy mistress some rich anger shows,
>   Emprison her soft hand, and let her rave,
>   And feed deep, deep upon her peerless eyes.
>
> She dwells with Beauty—Beauty that must die;
>   And Joy, whose hand is ever at his lips
> Bidding adieu; and aching Pleasure nigh,

Turning to poison while the bee-mouth sips:
Aye, in the very temple of Delight
   Veil'd Melancholy has her sovran shrine,
         Though seen of none save him whose
strenuous tongue
   Can burst Joy's grape against his palate fine;
His soul shalt taste the sadness of her might,
         And be among her cloudy trophies hung.

"That's exquisite, John," Fanny says.

"Thank you."

She picks up the paper, reads something, and makes a face. "However … what's this about 'beauty that must die'? What kind of a statement is that to make about the one you love?"

I take her hand and emprison it in my own.

"Your eyes truly are peerless," I tell her. "And your beauty—also without equal."

"I hope you love me for more than my 'beauty,' my dear boy." She strokes my hair.

"I do. But you can't blame me for being enraptured of it." I bend forward for another kiss.

"I believe there was never another poet like you, John Keats. But I want you to know, I love you for who you are as a man and not because you are a poet."

"Thank God for that," I declare. "I have met women who I really think would like to be married to a Poem and to be given away by a Novel."

She laughs and throws her arms around me. We roll about in the grass, talking and smooching. It is impossible for either of us to believe that our spring together will ever grow old and fade.

N

We rose higher into the sky, high enough again to see the curve of the earth's horizon. When the poet turned toward me then, I understood him well enough to know there was something he wanted to explain.

J

There are two words that describe my life, I announce to the little spirit. Two words so closely related, they share all their letters but one.

The spirit pulses to show it is listening.

Poetry and *poverty*. No sooner had Fanny Brawne and I rekindled our romance, no sooner had I begun again to write *poetry*, than I was forced by *poverty* to take leave of her. Summer was approaching, and Brown needed to rent out his half of Wentworth Place at a price I couldn't afford.

My money had dwindled away. From the sale of my poetry I earned almost nothing, and making matters worse, I'd allowed George to borrow from my share of the estate—what little remained—to finance his move with Georgina to Kentucky. And then the final straw: Abbey informed us that the estate was forbidden to release any more funds because of a legal challenge by a distant relative.

Poetry. Poverty.

The spirit pulses in sympathy.

⁂

$\mathcal{N}$

The poet and Fanny Brawne sat side by side, hand in hand, on the grass beneath the plum tree. "Fanny ... it was my deepest hope that you and I could have an understanding before I left for the summer."

She squeezed his hand and looked deeply into his eyes.

He sighed. "Yesterday, I learned it is impossible ... now, and for the foreseeable future. Abbey has informed us that the estate is tied up in legal action—probably for years. The truth is, Fanny, I am completely impoverished. I have nothing to offer you."

She pressed her finger to his lips, leaned forward, and kissed him.

"I never said you had to offer me anything but yourself," she murmured. She kissed him again. "We can wait."

The poet began to make a reply but stopped mid-word.

"What's wrong?"

"I thought I heard something move up there." He leaned back and spied up into the branches of my tree.

"Are you sure?" she asked, following his gaze. "I don't see anything."

"It must be my nightingale," he replied with a shrug.

But it was not his nightingale.

The poet and Fanny stood up and walked inside, hand in hand. A short time later, with a stealthy air, glancing about to see if anyone was watching, Margaret scurried down from her hiding place in the tree.

Mrs. Brawne met her at the door, and Margaret leaned forward and whispered something in her mother's ear. "Nothing to offer?" the mother asked. "Nothing at all?" Margaret nodded. The blood drained from Mrs. Brawne's face.

The next morning, the poet trudged through the yard carrying a large duffel bag. He set down the bag, ran back, and gave Fanny one final kiss before he boarded a coach and left. Mrs. Brawne looked on in silence, her arms folded on her chest.

Two months later, in a quiet town near a ragged coastline, the poet sat at a small table, pen in hand.

I love you too much to venture to Hampstead. Knowing well that my life must be passed in fatigue and trouble, I have been endeavoring to wean myself from you, but I cannot cease to love you.

The poet strolled through the town—down a cobbled lane, past a church, across a river on a slender wooden bridge, and out into a field. In a nearby grove of oaks and maples, the leaves gleamed red and yellow. Clouds glowed like heated stones in the western sky. A field of stubble warmed its feet in the radiant evening light.

J

(Remembering, reciting)

> Where are the songs of Spring? Ay, where are they?
>   Think not of them, thou hast thy music too,—
> While barred clouds bloom the soft-dying day,
>   And touch the stubble plains with rosy hue;
> Then in a wailful choir the small gnats mourn
>   Among the river sallows, borne aloft

Or sinking as the light wind lives or dies;
And full-grown lambs loud bleat from hilly bourn;
Hedge-crickets sing; and now with treble soft
The redbreast whistles from a garden-croft,
And gathering swallows twitter in the skies.

N

He could not cease to love her.

Early October, Hampstead. Margaret pulled open the front door and spun about. "Fanny!" she called shrilly. "It's him!"

Fanny approached, and Margaret shot past her.

Fanny came forward and took the poet's hands. Her hair was piled atop her head. Her eyes gazed deeply into his. She didn't offer a kiss.

"Would you like me to be cruel and distant to you, John?" she asked. "And try to wean myself from you?"

When he sought her eyes, she looked away.

Mrs. Brawne entered the room and greeted the poet from a chilly distance.

J

By autumn, Fanny and I have found our way to another dead end in the labyrinth. Meanwhile, Mrs. Brawne's feelings toward me have cooled for reasons I don't understand, and I can't leave soon enough to satisfy her.

I have run out of money and am desperate to secure an income. From Hampstead, I proceed directly to London to look for work. I hope to find employment writing for newspapers and magazines—theatrical reviews, book reviews, political musings—anything.

But all I find is poverty.

Staying in the cheapest lodgings in the seamiest parts of London, I spend each day passing from door to door along Fleet Street, searching for work.

Nothing.

I try all that month and the next. Still nothing.

A sore throat I contracted has hung on with a vengeance; the slightest hint of chill in the air makes me shiver. When the bitter cold descends in late fall, I find it helps to linger in front of a blacksmith's shop and soak in the heat from the glowing coals.

One night, I end up in the doorway of a butcher's shop, basking in the musky heat of dressed animals.

Someone stirs within.

"You again?" a voice growls from the back of the shop. A huge mass of a man shambles forward, wiping his arms on a dirty towel. "You're back, are you? Looking for a rematch, no doubt?"

I look up and see—yes. Him.

By now I am shivering uncontrollably. I sag against the doorjamb, too weak and cold even to think of raising my fists.

The butcher takes a few steps closer. For a long moment, he doesn't move. A strange expression comes over the slab of his face. He turns, disappears into the back of the shop, and returns with something wrapped in a piece of butcher paper.

"Take this," he growls, thrusting the package at me. Without a word, I accept it from him.

"Don't come back 'ere again expecting a handout," he mutters.

I stumble off down the street, gnawing at the bones.

XI

N

As we sailed higher, the earth revealed itself to be a blue sphere, round and complete, and I would have liked to feast my eyes on this remarkable sight. But there was no time to enjoy it, for Raven man floated into view, seated at his desk with pen in hand, smacking his lips as he jotted figures on a piece of parchment.

Do you approach me yet again, pleading poverty?

Why bother to speak, when everything you say is a lie?

How dare you make such an accusation to a man of dignity and honor!

Dignity and honor? You defrauded my family's estate.

Haven't we already determined that it's a bit too late to do anything?

Too late to do anything? Perhaps. But it's not too late for *nothing.*

For what?

For nothing.

For nothing?

Nothing. Like the Quaker's horse.

What is it you intend to do?

The poet pulled open a safe and reached inside. He drew out a large bag, fluffed it up, thrust an arm in, rooted around, and finally bent forward to peer inside. He stood up and shrugged.

After all that has happened, I still hoped that I might be wrong about the extent of your treachery. But, alas, no. I take it this is all that remains of my family's silver?

It is. Every last bit of it.

Raven man gurgled with pleasure as if preparing to settle onto the carcass of a rabbit. But a motion in the distance caught his eye, and he turned to observe a second visitor floating toward them out of the gloom.

It was Pigeon man, his thumbs tucked into his vest. He alighted next to Raven man and paced back and forth with an important air as he addressed the poet.

Have you forgotten about the payment you promised me?

The "payment" you refer to was a misunderstanding.

There was no misunderstanding. You made a promise.

I promised only that I would let you know when the money from my brother's estate was released.

You're splitting straws.

As it happened, the release of my brother's estate was delayed for years—and all because of the efforts of that villain whom you see seated beside you.

The "villain" opened his claws. *This is slander!*

If you delayed the release of the estate, kind sir, I have no doubt that you were simply doing your job with due diligence.

I was indeed. By the way, my good man, I am Richard Abbey, the tea merchant.

And I am Benjamin Haydon, the painter. Perhaps you have heard of my masterpiece, Christ's Entry into Jerusalem.

I regret to say that I have not. But I am pleased to meet you nonetheless.

Likewise.

The tea merchant delayed and delayed. And after months and months that turned into years and years, when the money was finally released, how much did I receive? The immense sum of sixty pounds.

All you're really saying is that your word is worth nothing.

I am certain that you deserve every bit of opprobrium that you receive—from me and from this honest soul before you.

You're a false friend, John Keats. You tricked me, and I have no doubt that you are guilty of tricking this fine gentleman as well.

I am well aware of my failings, but in my dealings with both of you I believe I was honest and fair. I cannot say the same of you.

Not honest and fair? Prove it! If you can!

I believe I can. May I again seek the intervention of a higher power?

J

I believe it is time, I announce to the heavens, *I believe it is time to seek again the verdict of the universe—this time a judgment regarding my dealings with these two gentlemen. Which of us was more honest and fair?*

N

There it was—that immense double-pan balance, its widespread arms poised in perfect symmetry. The majestic scale dwarfed the humans. Raven man clasped his hands to his heart, and Pigeon man's jaw dropped to his chest. They huddled together, trembling.

"Do you see it?" the poet demanded of Raven man. "The 'larger and more forbidding balance scale' with which you threatened us in your countinghouse."

J

I know now to expect the unexpected, so I am not surprised when I am lifted high into the gloom above the pan on the left. I find I am seated on something quite massive. Leaning forward and peering down, I see it is a splendid marble column that forms the shape of a capital *I*. The column and I remain a short distance above the pan.

Abbey and Haydon—casting fearful glances at each other—rise in the opposite direction and drift over the pan on the right, each seated like a small bug atop his own column.

"*I* for *integrity*," I conjecture.

N

Integrity seemed to mean honesty or fair play. The question to be settled was whose integrity was greater—the poet's or his two visitors'?

As soon as the twin columns bearing Raven man and Pigeon man touched down on the pan on the right, it sank several feet beneath their combined mass. They kicked and swung their legs like children, and Pigeon man was the first to speak.

That was quick!

It was indeed!

A judgment has been rendered in our favor.

Our lives of virtue and probity have been fully vindicated.

As we knew they would.

It was the righteousness of our cause.

Answer me now, John Keats. Do you see whose claims have more substance?

And whose actions have found favor in the all-seeing eyes of the benevolent God who rules over this universe?

The two men failed to see something, however. The poet had not yet settled into place on his pan but was still suspended above it. With no trace of hurry, like a maple seed, he drifted downward. And the moment his column touched the pan, it lurched down so violently that the other two men were catapulted into the air along with their columns, which spun off into the darkness.

Raven man sailed a fair distance, tipped, and tumbled headfirst toward an open bag that appeared to be waiting for him. He landed inside it like an egg plopping into a nest. The fit was so snug that nothing remained visible but his thin legs, wriggling.

J

Emprisoned in the money bag he loves so dearly, Abbey ascends into the night sky, describing a graceful parabola toward a distant star. Closer and closer he sails. For one brief moment, he and his money bag flare like a hot coal and then melt away into the cosmos, a dark and shapeless mass.

N

Pigeon man puffed up larger and shot straight up. As he inflated, his skin stretched tight as a drum. With a deafening pop, he burst into thousands of little pieces that fluttered off into the void, wriggling like maggots. From the haze of the explosion there emerged a much smaller and humbler creature in the shape of a tadpole, gazing back toward the poet, his tiny hands clasped before him.

J

Like a film of ice dissolving in a pool of water, the scale fades into the depths of the heavens.

XII

N

The poet's letter to George and Georgina about "the vale of soul-making" explained that "the heart must feel and suffer in a thousand diverse ways" to become a soul. That made sense, but the poet's description of the school and the "horn Book" was harder to follow.

Since finding myself in spirit form, I've felt some new ways myself. The poet's words have flooded through me like a rainstorm through a dry streambed.

At one time I was a bird, what he called a light-winged dryad. Then, because of him, because of his verse, I became a spirit—his spirit guide.

But did that explain the sense of incompleteness I still felt around him?

And why did I have no idea what would come next? Each moment now was like the birth of a new song, when you open your throat to the sky, waiting for unknown notes to spring to life.

J

My attending spirit is swishing against me like a dog trying to reaffirm its affection.

Spirit, your friendliness is unfounded. You have no reason to revere me. True, I have now received one positive judgment from the heavens, but it's hardly a verdict on my whole life, which I know full well was riddled with poor judgment and bad decisions.

You should fly off like my nightingale, up the hill and into the next valley-glade—go on, now, be off! There you can give voice to your song of joy, if joy is what dwells in your heart. I can't expect you to understand the pain and conflict that have dwelt so long in mine.

𝒩

My task now could not be clearer: to restore his faith in his writing. It wouldn't be a simple assignment, for the poet was in a hopeless state. And I still had no way to communicate with him.

A pulsing light can only give so much information.

As I brooded, I felt my mind fill with some of the verse he composed on that morning so long ago beneath the plum tree:

Light-winged Dryad of the trees.

With thee fade away into the forest dim.

On the viewless wings of Poesy.

The strange phrases pained my sense, filling me almost to overflowing.

I felt an ache in my heart.

A drowsy numbness in my head.

The ache gathered like a thundercloud—and burst into glorious joy.

The numbness stirred like a baby bird—and cracked open its shell.

I was quickened into motion, scattered into flight, dazzled into a burst of release and rejoicing. In the midst of all the darkness and gloom, I found myself dancing, flying, sparkling. And that was when it happened. Like a song welling up from the core of my being, a shower of words and phrases spilled out into the night.

The poet looked up. An inscription flashed upon the night like sunlight on a pool of water.

Summer.

J

Something very odd is taking place in the dusk around me. Like a dog in a state of frenzy, the spirit is dashing about, scattering phosphorescent trails that hang in the air like banners of light. And now, across these banners, lines and curves inscribe themselves, like a pen on paper, and reveal themselves to be the shapes of letters and words.

Summer.

Fever.

It is not long before a litany of phrases is suspended around me in the darkness.

Light-winged Dryad of the trees.

With thee fade away into the forest dim.

On the viewless wings of Poesy.

The murmurous haunt of flies on summer eves.

Easeful Death.

Thou wast not born for death, immortal Bird!

Fled is that music:—do I wake or sleep?

I know the phrases, of course—they are from my "Ode to a Nightingale." But why, at this moment, should I be compelled to look upon them again?

Am I being taunted for my failures?

I know all too well that this poem, like all my poems, failed to find even the most modest readership. Immediately upon publication, it sank back into the sea of words that batter Britain's shores.

The spirit has ventured closer, as if hoping to perch on my shoulder. I turn away and shake my head, pleading for solitude.

N

He was still tormented by so much. His failed poetry. His doomed love.

All that rejoicing, all that energy—and it did no good. But it was a start. I had found a way to write words.

Could I write something different, something better—something that might ease his soul?

Maybe, just maybe, I thought, if the poet could understand the depth of Fanny's love for him, he wouldn't consider himself such a failure. Maybe, if he could be convinced of the power of his words to transform his readers, he might feel some measure of success.

It was time for the next step. Dance, fly, sparkle ... with a message designed to lift his heart.

J

The spirit is whirling around me again, trailing streams of phosphorescence. This time, mercifully, no words inscribe themselves. The spirit slows down and glides back toward me, as if disappointed or confused.

N

I danced, I flew, I sparkled, and as I did so, I formed two pure thoughts in my mind: *Fanny Brawne still loves you* and *Your poetry has changed me—forever.*

Nothing happened. No words inscribed themselves in the ether.

A second time I tried, whirling around the poet, throwing off sparkles of light and filling myself to overflowing with the thought *Your verse will live forever in the hearts of men and women.*

Again, nothing happened.

I tried once more, desperate to discover what worked. This time, instead of my own thoughts, I again conjured up one of the poet's verses.

J

The spirit makes yet another mad dash around me, and now some letters take shape around us. Inscribing themselves in the trail of light are the words *Tender is the night.*

Another phrase to taunt me.

N

I was beginning to understand my limitations. I could only summon up words or phrases that came directly from the poet's verse.

This wouldn't do much good if he felt mocked by them. But I wondered—could there be a way to take his words and reshape them into a different message, one he might welcome?

To do that, I'd need to draw on every bit of skill I possessed.

One of nightingales' greatest powers is our ability to weave fragments of sound into a new and complex song. We pick and choose from what is in us and around us and combine it in fresh and clever ways.

That skill could prove useful now.

In the same way a parent gathers choice leaves and pieces of straw for a nest, I could sort through the poet's words and pluck out phrases that would deliver the message I wanted to give him.

A message of hope.

J

If I had given up writing poetry as any reasonable man might have done, I could have found happiness and love with Fanny Brawne. But, of course, I carried on in my stubborn way.

And now, adding to the misery of my failings, I am accosted by a new set of words writing themselves in the dusk.

They appear to come from one of my poems—but altered.

Missing phrases. Strange gaps in syntax. What could be the reason for this abomination?

> *Ode*
>
> *A heart had sunk*
> *in shadows numberless.*
>
> *Forget the weariness and sorrow*
> *for I fly to thee,*
> *with the breezes blown*
> *through the darkness.*

Death with no pain,
In ecstasy sing!

The voice charm'd like a bell.
Thy plaintive anthem
cannot fade.

Wake.

Random words from my "Ode to a Nightingale" turned to a hopeless mishmash.

Why, spirit, why?

N

Abomination. A hopeless mishmash.

My talents aren't equal to the task.

I can't deny I'm simpleminded when compared to him. My thoughts next to his are plain and artless. I lack the depth and the gravity of his melancholy.

I am still a nightingale. Though I've been transported to this place and changed, I haven't left behind my basic nature. If given the option, I'd still choose a melodious plot of beechen green over verdurous glooms.

I still hope that every journey through darkness will end in light. I still prefer joy to despair.

My message to the poet has only upset him. But I have to try again. Somewhere between our two natures, can't we find a meeting place?

J

The spirit has withdrawn to a modest distance and is pulsing to call my attention to a new set of words glimmering in the dusk.

> *Friend of all,*
> *bless with sweet days*
> *whoever seeks thee.*

> *Steady, patient songs.*
> *Thy music lives*
> *in the skies.*

> *Joy is nigh.*

I recognize the origins of these phrases in my verse, but again, my original meaning has been cropped away, leaving a jumbled message.

"Joy is nigh?" A fond notion indeed.

XIII

J

Poverty has two close companions, pain and illness. Both are un-invited guests, and once they arrive, both linger as long as they will.

I pray you, spirit, leave off your scribblings in the ether. Show me where I learned about the dread logic of pain, about the compound of opposites. Show me Dr. Cooper.

N

A small, cramped room. A flock of humans in white cloaks surrounded a nearly naked man splayed out on his back, bound by straps to a long table. One of those dressed in white was the poet. Another was a tall man with a mane of lustrous hair. He spoke now in a bold, brisk manner.

"Pain is a part of life, Mr. Keats, there's no need to fear it." He waved his blade toward the poet and the others who were gathered around him. "Life is a compound of opposites, and we can have no benefits in this world without some suffering, eh?"

"Yes, Dr. Cooper," the poet replied as he affixed a series of straps around the chest of the victim on the table. One of the other white cloaks secured a vise around the leg. The victim's foot dangled from the end of the table like a dead rat.

Suddenly and with no warning, Dr. Cooper took a step forward, seized the man's foot, and sliced off the end of it, then used another tool to pry off the mangled bones. The victim's screams roared through the empty hallways and echoed off the walls of nearby buildings. Passersby outside the hospital gripped their coats and hurried on. The poet gritted his teeth and tightened the straps one more notch.

J

I feel the verge of my own chapter of pain and horror: the onset of my illness.

It tested my most cherished beliefs.

For all my musings to George and Georgina about the vale of soul-making, I found little then that was redemptive. It is the privilege of the healthy to spout such notions.

The desperately sick can only creep forward beneath the weight of their daily suffering.

And the daily struggle to keep love steady in the heart.

N

The sound of pounding hooves. Frosty heaves of breath. The top of a rattling stagecoach, where the poet rode in the open air, hunched over, shivering in the cold. He wore no hat or topcoat, and his lips were blue as a jay. By the time they reached Hampstead, his face shone pale and ghastly. He alighted from the coach and stumbled into the house.

Charles Brown heard the uneven steps.

"Have you been drinking? What in God's name is the matter with you ..." he began, but stopped as he caught sight of the poet, supporting himself against a wall. "You are fevered, John?"

The poet turned his head slightly. "A bit," he admitted. "To save money, I rode on top of the coach."

"That was foolish."

"Poverty makes fools of us all."

"You must go to bed at once."

The poet gave a faint nod and started up the stairs.

Brown poured out a glass of liquid and brought it to the poet, who had already changed into his bedclothes and was climbing into bed.

As he entered the cold sheets, even before his head was on the pillow, the poet coughed, and something rushed into his throat.

He touched his lips with his fingers and saw the red stain upon them.

"Are you all right?" Brown asked.

"I am thinking of Fanny," the poet muttered. He drew in a great gasp of air, shuddering. "Of Fanny. I am afraid I may never—" He didn't finish the thought.

Brown waited a minute and then tapped his shoulder. "You are better now?"

The poet leaned over and peered down at something. "This is unfortunate." He nodded toward the sheets. "That is blood from my mouth."

J

"Bring me the candle, Brown," I order him, "and let me see this blood."

Brown holds the candle higher and presses in beside me. I gaze steadfastly at the single drop on the sheets.

"I know the color," I tell him. "It is arterial blood; I cannot be deceived. That drop of blood is my death warrant—I must die."

> This living hand, now warm and capable
> Of earnest grasping, would, if it were cold

And in the icy silence of the tomb,
So haunt thy days and chill thy dreaming nights
That thou would wish thine own heart dry of blood
So in my veins red life might stream again,
And thou be conscience-calm'd—see here it is
I hold it towards you.

N

I turned my head away.

J

My love for Fanny Brawne rescues me from despair. All our troubles with each other from earlier that autumn have scattered with the leaves. Though at first we aren't allowed to see each other, we write notes back and forth, several each day. Finally, a week after the hemorrhage, she can visit. It's lovely to have her sit beside me for the evening, talking and knitting.

Over the next weeks, some strength returns. There's no more time to waste.

When she arrives that evening, Fanny stops just inside the door. In the depths of her blue eyes I see a flash of comprehension, but she tries not to let on. "Look at you, John Keats—fully dressed, and seated in a chair! Are you on your way to a dance? Perhaps a dinner out with friends?"

There is no need for words. With effort, I steady myself on one knee before her and unfold my hands to reveal the treasure I've been saving for her, dear to me though not dear in price—a garnet ring in a setting of gold. Also in the box, folded neatly, is the poem I composed for her.

I press my lips to her hand, and with our eyes and with our hearts, we declare our love to each other.

Can her family understand the depth of our commitment? For now, we vow to keep the engagement secret.

> Bright star, would I were steadfast as thou art!
>   Not in lone splendour hung aloft the night,
> And watching, with eternal lids apart,
>   Like Nature's patient, sleepless Eremite,
> The moving waters at their priestlike task
>   Of pure ablution round earth's human shores,
> Or gazing on the new soft fallen mask
>   Of snow upon the mountains and the moors:
> No—yet still steadfast, still unchangeable,
>   Pillow'd upon my fair love's ripening breast,
> To feel for ever its soft swell and fall,
>   Awake for ever in a sweet unrest,
> Still, still to hear her tender-taken breath,
> And so live ever—or else swoon to death.

N

Fanny Brawne left for London to visit the Dilkeses, and the poet's illness took a turn for the worse.

J

Those few weeks when Fanny is off in London, I lie alone in

my bed. My fever returns and my thoughts run wild. Images of Fanny's independent life frolic in my imagination. I see her in the grey dress that hugs the curve of her hips, or the black formal gown that bares her beautiful shoulders. She stands in a large, elegant hall that is brilliantly lit by candles. Handsome young officers take note of her and make comments about her, exchanging sly winks with one another. They approach her and make stylish bows, and she accepts their invitations to dance. She is in their arms, smiling and laughing, making witty comments. Roses blush on her cheeks. With the handsomest officer of all, she strolls out onto a balcony, arm in arm. He is healthy and from a well-connected family, brimming with the confidence that social status affords to even the most dull. He inclines his face toward hers, and she—

Through friends in London, I hear rumors of a certain lieutenant who has caught Fanny's eye, and I have a hemorrhage of emotion not unlike the earlier hemorrhage of my lungs.

My Sweet Love,

You could not step or move an eyelid but it would shoot to my heart—I am greedy of you. Do not think of anything but me. Your going to town alone, when I heard of it was a shock to me—yet I expected it—promise me you will not for some time, till I get better. Confess if your heart is too much fasten'd on the world. If you would really what is call'd enjoy yourself at a Party—if you can smile in people's faces and wish them to admire you now, you never have nor ever will love me—I see life in nothing but the certainty of your

Love—convince me of it my sweetest. If I am not somehow convinc'd I shall die of agony. If we love we must not live as other men and women do—I cannot brook the wolfsbane of fashion and foppery and tattle. You must be mine to die upon the rack if I want you. My recovery of bodily health will be of no benefit to me if you are not all mine when I am well. For God's sake save me—or tell me my passion is of too awful a nature for you. Again God bless you.

    J.K.

"You must be mine to die upon the rack if I want you." I shudder now to think I wrote those words.

Do you see now, spirit—do you see why she had no reason to keep on loving me, and why you have no reason now to show me kindness? Whatever befalls me in this way station where we find ourselves, I am fully deserving.

N

To which I replied in my mind, Not so fast. The course of true love never did run smooth.

J

The summer returns, and once again, I have to leave Brown's house. I take a room with my friend, the poet Leigh Hunt, in Kentish Town, but after a few weeks I fall into a steep decline. Because of my illness, very little oxygen is now reaching my brain—perhaps that's why I grow so despondent. A letter from Fanny arrives; a nosy servant slips it open and reads it before bringing it to me. Incensed at this breach of privacy, I barge out the door and stagger outside.

N

Drawing on the last of his strength, the poet set out on the walk of several miles to Hampstead. Late that night, out of breath, shivering with cold, he arrived at the home of the Brawnes.

He lurched up to the door and gave a feeble knock, leaning against the wall for support.

Margaret pulled the door open and gasped.

"Momma!" she called. "It's John Keats, and he's feverish and ill!"

When Mrs. Brawne came to the door and saw the poet, her hand shot to her mouth.

"My darling John, you must come in and lie down immediately!" she exclaimed, reaching forward to guide him inside.

Fanny came running up. "Oh, John!" she cried. She gave him a quick peck on the cheek, and she and her mother led him into the guest room and settled him in bed.

J

It is an irony almost too deep to bear. For the first time, I am living in the same flat as Fanny. She is close at hand, no longer separated from me by a wall. But I am here as an invalid, nothing more. And my imagination is still too strong, my sense of reality still too sharp, for me to pretend that a greater separation does not loom over us.

The Brawnes nurse me and care for me as I await the ship that will carry me to Italy, whose warm climate (so say the doctors) is my only hope for surviving the winter.

Each day, Fanny and I talk for hours. Together, we lay out our plans. I will go to Italy with my friend Joseph Severn, a painter who has offered to accompany me and care for me. In the favorable Mediterranean climate, I will recover my health. Fanny gives me a carnelian, a small white gemstone, for good luck. Once my convalescence is complete, I will return to Hampstead, and she and I will marry. For a time, we will live with her family; then we will set up our own household and raise a family. I will write and teach. She will be a fashion designer like her famous cousin, Beau Brummell. We will raise our children in the fullness of our love, and when all is done, we will spend our final years, grey and doting on each other, in a cottage by the sea.

$\mathcal{N}$

One evening, Fanny Brawne asked her mother to come sit with her in the parlor.

"Should I leave?" Margaret asked.

"No, you may stay," Fanny told her.

Mrs. Brawne seated herself next to her older daughter.

"Mother ..." Fanny took a deep breath. "John and I are engaged. Once he recovers, he will return to England, and we will marry." She gave a quick glance toward her mother.

"I see," Mrs. Brawne replied in a calm voice.

"There's no sense in opposing this, Mother. Our minds are made up."

Mrs. Brawne stirred in her chair. "I have no intention of opposing it," she replied.

Fanny's blue eyes turned again to her mother.

Mrs. Brawne patted her hand. "I give you both my full blessing."

Margaret watched and listened, wide-eyed.

Fanny hugged her mother and bowed her head, weeping. As she pulled away, she said, "It's still a secret, Mother—still a secret except for those of us in this house."

"Of course, dear," her mother replied. With an expression neither joyous nor sad, she watched her daughter stand and leave the room.

"Mother," Margaret asked as she was climbing into bed, "how can you agree to their engagement? You know John has no money and no prospects ... and now he is ill ... and you've said many times we can't continue to live in poverty."

Mrs. Brawne smoothed out the covers over her.

"It won't happen," she remarked quietly.

A quick intake of breath. "What do you mean it won't happen?"

"Shhh!" her mother warned, glancing toward the door. She sat down beside her younger daughter and touched her hair. "It won't happen ... because John won't be coming back from Rome."

Margaret gazed into her mother's face for a moment, then lowered her head and burst into tears.

The next day, September 17, 1820, the poet took a coach to London and boarded the ship for Italy.

XIV

J

My bedroom overlooks the Spanish Steps and a splashing fountain. As death prepares to draw me into its arms, doubt holds my heart captive. I can't bear even to open the last three letters Fanny Brawne sends to me in Rome.

N

Flickering like a flame, the young woman clothed in leaves appeared again before us.

Please, John, I must tell you something.

Fanny, haven't we both suffered enough?

In your thoughts—in your doubts and misgivings—you do not see me as I am. I implore you to look into my eyes and accept the truth of what you find there.

They stood and gazed at each other.

⁂

My responsibility was clear: to find the truth about Fanny Brawne and communicate it to the poet, however I could.

Nightingales are ground birds who root through dried stalks and grasses for bugs and worms and other foods. I could make use of that skill now in sorting through the remnants of his life.

A life that has passed settles into place like layers of leaves, the residue of all that was, a record of time and place and event.

Unlike leaves, which crumble and decay, a life's residue remains for those who know where and how to look.

I dove into the ether and trusted to the purity of my quest. I plunged deep and true and worked my way through many and various layers, through sounds and images and light and shadow, and finally I came to the time and place in question—the poet's life and the lives of those he loved.

First, I had to find out if his fears were justified. When Fanny went to town alone, was her heart too much fastened on the world? Did she flirt with handsome officers and find pleasure in their arms at parties and dances?

The truths that I uncovered were not encouraging. To each of those questions, the answer was the same. Yes.

There was a certain young lieutenant by the name of James Reed. He was tall and rather formal in his demeanor. But his smile was warm and charming. He danced with grace and skill and a winning air of deference. The scrupulous attention he showed Fanny captured her fancy.

There was a meeting between them on the balcony, much as the poet had imagined. Worse than he imagined. Reed invited Fanny for a walk in the garden through the soft, fragrant evening. The glories of spring echoed from the trees. Robins sang in rapture, blackbirds squawked and tumbled. His arm about her waist, the scent of his easy masculinity, the stirrings within her, seemed to exist in a world of their own, separate from her life with John Keats. A license was granted in the half light of the moon. Reed and Fanny wandered in the garden for half an hour and exchanged a number of sweet kisses.

Did she still love John Keats? She did. She was young and more than capable, as the young and earthbound are, of feeling many things at once. She was still a few months short of her twentieth birthday—quite young for a human.

It cannot be denied that her visits to the city ruffled the nest of her love for John Keats. For a few perilous days, her heart wavered.

But then it steadied and found its true course.

In the week following the rendezvous in the garden, she was overcome with a strong emotion—regret. At the next dance, she declined the attentions of the handsome Lieutenant Reed. She vowed not to cross that line again, no matter how delightful and charming the suitor. She chose, once and for all, to honor her love for John Keats.

She would never betray him again.

᷍᷍᷍

I returned from my quest, pulsing with the good news I'd discovered. But there was no disturbing the two lovers.

After gazing into each other's eyes for an eternity that lasted an instant, John Keats and Fanny Brawne came together in a kiss that enveloped them both in a glow like starlight. Then, slowly and all at once, she flared into the darkness like a flame folding into its own source of warmth.

J

The kiss is heavenly—how could it be otherwise—but can I believe the love of such a phantom? Or is this merely another trick to deceive me?

Before I can give this further thought, the writing again scrolls around me, so insistent I have no choice but to respond.

Bright Star. Steadfast.

Simple spirit, methinks you doth protest too much. She was not steadfast.

Steadfast.

Would that she had been so.

Still steadfast.

You have no proof.

Still unchangeable.

I know she loved me once. But how would you describe the state of her love now?

Eternal.

You expect me to believe that?

Eternal. Unchangeable.

I see no reason why I should believe your words, which—in any event—are really *my* words turned inside out.

Feel her sweet unrest. Her tender breath.

You seem sincere, and I don't doubt your kind intent. But I question the quality of your knowledge.

Glut thy sorrow. Burst Joy's grape.

After a life that ended so miserably?

Joy is nigh.

When all around me are strewn my failures and disappointments?

Think not of them.

No great epic. No great love. No stirring message of hope for the people I left behind in this vale of soul-making.

Be conscience-calm'd.

Kind spirit, will even a single verse of mine live past the day of my death?

And with that, the spirit launches into a frenzied flight.

N

I thought at first I would try something new: to form the trailing bands of light into shapes and likenesses that would, once and for all, dispel his doubts. Images of book upon book, volume upon volume, of all sizes and types, piled high like rich garners bursting with grain: bound in leather, covered in cloth, small enough to be held in one hand, large enough to support the rookery of a stork.

And all bearing the name of their renowned author: John Keats.

But in midflight, I stopped. Such a revelation would be too cheap, too easy—and unworthy of his genius.

John Keats needed to find his own salvation or none at all. There had to be another way.

I hovered at a fair distance, considering, and then I etched one more phrase in the ether.

See here it is, I hold it towards you.

J

Hold what towards me? I see nothing, gentle spirit. Where are the proofs that my poetry shall live?

Ay, where are they?

No more taunting! Where is the evidence?

Already with thee!

Wicked spirit, you toy with me. Can we drop the disguises? Will you tell me who the devil you are?

With that, the light dims. The letters fade. Dusk settles in around us, deep and dark. All that is left of the spirit is a faint pulse of light somewhere in the distance.

Spirit? Spirit! Where have you gone?

My question echoes in the void.

Then slowly, with the shyness of an otter, the spirit advances through the air. Its light pulses softly, like that of a murky creature rising from the depths of the sea.

Tell me who you are. Spirit, I command you.

The light flickers and returns. The letters inscribe their legend on the face of the night.

Dryad.

Dryad?

Light-winged Dryad.

Are you saying that you are—?

Light-winged Dryad of the trees.

My nightingale? You are my nightingale?

Immortal Bird!

Then you are not a vision?

Or a waking dream.

You are my nightingale—in spirit form?

Light-winged Dryad.

But what could be your purpose?

To bless thy songs.

Did my poem give you life?

Forever.

And my poetry?

Thou wast not born for death.

It too will live?

Forever.

I find your hopeful thoughts difficult to accept.

But no matter.

I am convinced that we have finally arrived at the end point, the moment when all must be decided.

N

I wondered if he was ready. But with no hesitation, he raised his head toward the heavens.

J

I submit myself—the sum total of everything, my life and my work—to the judgment of the universe.

As soon as I make this declaration, the spirit zips off into the ether—and returns with the terrible contraption that will determine my final fate. Watching its approach, I still don't know if this instrument of justice exists on its own, apart from me, or is merely the manifestation of my own self-doubt and regrets.

Can both be true?

N

For the third time, the colossal pan balance appeared before us, gleaming silver and gold, soaring high above us into the heavens. The poet and I looked on in silence. Had we indeed reached the final judgment that would determine his fate? And in the end, would his immortal poetry tip the scales in his favor?

It seemed clear that his life and work—the sum of his accomplishments and successes—would fill one pan. But what would be placed upon the other? What were the failures against which they would be weighed?

It wasn't long before the answer revealed itself. On the pan to our left rested two separate images, both quite large. One was a cameo of the poet's face in profile, complete with the overhang of his upper lip over the lower, rendered in raised relief against a pale background of seashell or stone. The other was the leather cover of a book with the legend *The Complete Poems and Letters of John Keats*. Over both was suspended a large *V*, as blue and resplendent as a cloudless summer sky.

J

V for virtue.

N

On the right pan, in a messy heap, writhed a myriad of images. Some were known to me already. A young girl crying in her bedroom. A pigeon man holding out a hand for money. A stick man stretched on a bed. A bald man frowning as he holds up a vial of amber liquid. Others, less familiar, wriggled among them, jostling for space. A man dressed in black with a medical instrument around his neck, looking about as if in need of assistance. A woman with a crudely painted face that could not conceal deep lines of worry, lounging against a crumbling brick wall in an alleyway. A large matron by a meat locker, peering down in surprise at an empty shelf. A young woman pinioned on a rack. And others, too unsavory and numerous to mention.

The *V* above these images was red, the color of blood.

J

V for vice.

N

The two pans were now full, their contents in place. The immense scale commenced its motion up and down as it prepared to render judgment. First the pan on the left descended, but then it was lifted smoothly and steadily as the scale on the right sank down below its departure point. But even then, we weren't done. The two pans went back and forth, up and down, wrestling for dominance, with neither one declaring itself the winner.

And so it continued for some time. The motions grew less and less discernible, and finally both pans came to a stop—in perfect balance.

Neither side had triumphed. There had been no judgment.

XV

N

Something new made its appearance. In the space over the pan on the left, atop the blue *V* for *virtue,* there appeared the outline of a bird with a question mark inscribed upon its breast. The same image also appeared atop the red *V* for *vice* over the pan on the right.

The poet turned and regarded me in silence for a moment. Then he shook his head and mused, "Is it possible, my friend, that you hold the missing piece that will complete the making of my soul?"

J

"Was it because of our ode?" I continue. "Or was it something I did—something perhaps that's been long buried in the welter of my life? Something I may shudder to recall?"

N

Shudder. The word struck me a swift blow. It's not a friendly word. What causes a shudder? Surprise or fear. A pang of cold. A deep regret.

I knew of no particular time in the poet's life that would make him shudder. But, as it happened, there had been one moment that made *me* shudder—for reasons I still didn't understand. It occurred when Charles Brown and the poet were strolling across the lawn toward my plum tree.

Did that stroll hide something of weight and importance—possibly the missing piece in his soul?

I recalled the curious message our mother once communicated to us concerning the poet—that he was our true friend, the best friend we would ever find among the earthbound.

What had he done? Could that have been the moment?

It was time to revisit the meeting between the poet and Charles Brown, when the poet behaved so oddly—when he gave a shove that almost threw Brown off his feet—and caused a *shudder* in the core of my being.

It deserved a closer look.

It is a windy and overcast day, with a dull glare that reduces the pupils of Brown's eyes to grains of black rice.

"The plan is to hike due north, through the Lake Country, and into Scotland," he says. "With a side trip to Ireland if possible." They are striding in the direction of my plum tree—though somehow I know I am not yet alive.

"That sounds splendid," the poet murmurs, tagging along. "Absolutely splendid."

"You are interested, no doubt, in making the acquaintance of the scenic hills and lakes that have so inspired William Wordsworth," Brown observes.

"I am," the poet confirms. "Seeing—experiencing—that landscape has become my passion." He gazes off into the distance—but his eyes cloud over, and he sighs.

A nightingale flits by, then returns for another close pass.

As he marches through some bushes and toward the tree, Brown holds up his hands to frame its stout trunk. He turns to the poet and opens his mouth to speak but is interrupted as the nightingale zips past them yet again—very close this time. My heart flutters as I realize who she is.

The poet looks up toward the sky, then down toward the ground ...

Suddenly he notices something remarkable. The nest of a bird is tucked in a tangle of undergrowth, and inside the nest he can see three small, olive-green eggs. Another step and Brown's large boots will crush them to bits.

Over the past weeks and months, the poet has experienced too much suffering not to feel a tremor at the core of his being.

"I want you to observe the bark of my plum tree—the way it cracks into exquisite little diamond patterns almost like the scales of a big—"

It is the impulse of a moment—too quick for conscious planning—the kind of act that reveals the true nature of a soul.

Brown gives a surprised grunt as he feels himself being shoved roughly to the side.

By the time he regains his balance, the poet has turned away and is facing someone entirely new: a young lady who strolls easy as a partridge across the grass in their direction. She wears a dress the color of leaves.

"Do grown men have nothing better to do than jostle each other about like little children?" she calls.

Brown spins toward her. "Oh, hello, Miss Brawne."

She stops short of them. "Good day, Mr. Brown. Who is your violent young friend?"

"John Keats, the poet," Brown says.

"The poet and pugilist, it seems," she adds, with a twist of her mouth.

"He is thinking of accompanying me on my hike north this summer, while your family rents my flat."

"You may want to reconsider that," she advises him. "It seems quite possible he might knock you off a mountaintop for sport and watch you topple down the slope."

The poet draws his hands apart and opens his mouth, but finds himself unable to give voice to his thoughts. He is, in fact, almost without breath.

J

The spirit floats over, hovers a few seconds in front of me as if wishing it could speak, and then flutters off toward the balance scale. It rises into the ether, and with a delicate motion of its beak traces the outlines of three small ovals. They fill in with an olive-green hue, shape themselves into solids, and slowly descend onto the pan on the left that contains a cameo of my face and a volume of my verse.

N

I allowed myself to drift away from the scale and back to the poet, watching all the while to see what, if anything, would come to pass.

At first, there was no change. On such a massive balance, laden with objects of such great size and bulk, the little eggs seemed too insignificant even to register.

The poet was watching it all intently.

"I had forgotten about those eggs," he said in a quiet and reverent tone.

And then it happened. A golden light rippled across the huge metal structure, and the pan on the left descended one small notch—and remained there.

The blue *V* for *virtue* bloomed like a musk rose, and the poet looked up with calm expectation in his eyes.

J

Like a spent wave slipping back into the sand, the balance scale dissolves into the heavens. My spirit guide pulses two or three times like a firefly, and I turn toward it and place my hands over my heart, which has somehow found its way back into my chest and is beating with tender insistence.

"Thank you, gentle spirit," I say, and the little spirit pulses one last time.

N

There was much for me to puzzle out—all the debts and acts of kindness. The tug I had felt, the unknown debt I had owed him, was nothing less than my life itself. The poet's quick action—one of tens or hundreds of small and unremarked moments on any given day—had saved my life, had made it possible. My life, in turn, had led early one morning many months later to the birth of his most beloved poem.

My debt to him, and his to me, were in balance.

And as great as they were, it wasn't his poems that had tipped the eternal scale.

In the end, what secured the poet's release was nothing greater—and nothing less—than the rescue of three tiny eggs.

XVI

𝒩

It was something we both felt. It was time.

Thank you—for everything.

𝒥

Spirit, our hearts in sympathy, we sense the moment of transition is upon us. I can never repay your kindness. May you always sing of summer in full-throated ease.

𝒥 & 𝒩

Adieu, my friend.

Adieu.

𝒥

It is one piece of suffering too many.

Outside the window, the pallid light of late January scatters like ashes on the Spanish Steps. Inside, lying in my bed in my little room at 26 Piazza di Spagna, I recoil from the sight of an envelope.

It is the last letter I will receive from Fanny Brawne.

"No, Severn—take it away. Take it out of my sight!" I protest. I am so weak, so delirious with lack of oxygen, that I can hardly speak. Reading Fanny's words now, when I have no chance of ever seeing her again, would be an agony too deep to bear.

I hold in my palm the smooth, delicate carnelian she gave me shortly before I left.

Over the next few weeks, I indicate my wishes for the burial, and I leave explicit orders with Severn: The grave should not bear my name; it shall read simply, "Here lies one whose name was writ in water." Fanny's three unopened letters will be buried beside me, along with a lock of her hair. I compose my final letter—it is to Charles Brown—and explain, "I have an habitual feeling of my real life having past, and that I am leading a posthumous existence." I close with a sentence that I know is the last I will ever write: "I can scarcely bid you good bye even in a letter. I always made an awkward bow."

In my final days, I ask for all my books to be brought into the room and piled around me, and they work like a charm. But my happy musings are interrupted. Around four in the afternoon on February 23, a great rush of blood comes into my throat, and I know that the end is upon me.

"Severn—I—lift me up—I am dying—I shall die easy—don't be frightened—be firm, and thank God it has come!"

N

Slowly, with dreamlike majesty, he rises into the sky, borne aloft by a hot-air balloon that is also the sun. It lifts him high above the peninsula of Italy and carries him across the austere beauty of the Alps and over the arid Spanish plains. Through rents in the clouds, he catches glimpses of the frothy blue expanse of the Atlantic. He comes to a new and wilder land, and the balloon starts to descend. Dusky green hills rise to meet him. A great river reveals itself. A simple brown bird greets him with a song he remembers from somewhere, full-throated and undying. The notes tumble from the sky and transform themselves into a path of garden stones, along which he walks with an ease that he has not felt in years. He does not know where he is, but his soul, forged in beauty and suffering, is capable of being in uncertainties. He is unsure if he wakes or sleeps.

The End

Poetic Texts

All poems and letters quoted in the novel are from:

The Complete Poetical Works and Letters of John Keats
Edited by Horace E. Scudder
©1899
Cambridge Edition
Boston and New York

Houghton Mifflin Company
The Riverside Press, Cambridge
Copyright 1899 by Houghton, Mifflin and Co.
All Rights Reserved

Except for "This Living Hand"
(from a facsimile of the manuscript)

Background Texts

Of all the biographical and critical writings I consulted on John Keats, the works I found most informative were two critical biographies: *John Keats* by Walter Jackson Bate (1963) and *Keats* by Andrew Motion (1997)—two works of scholarship with deep insights into Keats's life and writing. While I sometimes didn't agree with their interpretations of events in Keats's life or of the poetry, these two biographies have set the bar for any subsequent look at Keats's life.

Acknowledgments

This book went through a number of incarnations as it worked toward its final form. Thank you to my readers for helping me understand what to keep and what to trim.

My first and greatest thanks go, as always, to my wife, Barbara Elder. Among her many gifts is knowing when to voice candid judgments and when simply to offer the mercy of encouragement. Readers Kathy Butterworth, Pat Jones, Steven Sulzer, Keith Boynton, and Joe Blatt were also extremely generous with their insightful feedback, over more than one early draft.

Molly Best Tinsley, my editor, stepped in at a crucial point a few years into the project and encouraged me to look beyond the literal recreation of Keats's life—to allow myself the freedom to find new ways to engage with the material. My resulting explorations led to setting the story at the moment of Keats's death and to the twin narrators, Keats and the nightingale, thereby opening a number of luminous windows into Keats's universe. Thank you, Molly, for your brilliant editing.

Thanks also to Karetta Hubbard of Fuze Publishing for believing in the project, to Holly Moirs for her careful final edit, and to Ray Rhamey for his expert book design, which marshals an array of fonts and styles to keep the narrators and story in line.

Thanks finally to all those readers who still—two hundred years after his death—cherish and find delight in the poetry of John Keats, that most remarkable and lovable of poets.

Allusions

Some allusions to Keats and other writers appear unacknowl-
edged within the novel and are listed here by page number:

p. 3

"Cockney poet," etc. The comments by the three critics,
here and elsewhere in the novel, are direct (or slightly edited)
quotes from *Blackwood's Edinburgh Magazine* during and just
after Keats's life. These passages are thought to be the work of
John Gibson Lockhart and his associates.

The velocipede was something of a fad at the time, though
Keats dismissed it in a letter in the spring of 1819 to George and
Georgina as "the nothing of the day ... It is a wheel-carriage to
ride cock horse upon, sitting astride and pushing it along with
the toes, a rudder wheel in hand." It resembled a bicycle with
no pedals and soon fell out of favor. Bicycles with pedals came
decades later.

p. 4

The comments of the young woman are paraphrases from
statements in Keats's letters.

p. 4

"I mean to rely upon my abilities as a poet" is a statement that Abbey later claimed Keats made to him during the meeting in which Keats announced he was giving up his career as a surgeon in order to be a poet.

p. 5

"Nothing ever becomes real till it is experienced."

From Keats's letter to George and Georgina, February 14, 1819

p. 6

"posthumous existence"

From Keats's letter to Charles Brown, November 30, 1820: "I have an habitual feeling of my real life having past, and that I am leading a posthumous existence."

p. 6

"scattered like a pack of cards"

Rewording of "like a pack of scattered cards" from Keats's letter to Shelley, August 16, 1820

p. 6, 21, 25

"number me" or "be among the English poets"

Paraphrase of "I think I shall be among the English Poets after my death" from Keats's letter to George and Georgina, October 25, 1818

p. 9

    "You have led me on step by step, day by day."

    Part of a note from Haydon to Keats, April 12, 1819

p. 15

> As from the darkening gloom a silver dove
> Upsoars, and darts into the Eastern light,
> On pinions that naught moves but pure delight;
> So fled thy soul into the realms above.

    From Keats's "Sonnet: As From the Darkening Gloom a Silver Dove"

p. 19

    "Well," she whispers, "if it is born in us, how can we help it?"

    From Keats's letter to George and Thomas, January 5, 1818

p. 20

    "Well, John, I have read your book and it reminds me of the Quaker's horse which was hard to catch and good for nothing when he was caught. So your book is hard to understand and good for nothing when it is understood."

    Paraphrase of interview of Richard Abbey in 1820s by John Taylor

p. 21

"It is a better and a wiser thing to be a starved apothecary than a starved poet; so back to the shop Mr John, back to the plasters, pills, and ointment boxes ... But be a little more sparing of soporifics in your practice than you have been in your poetry."

From *Blackwood's Edinburgh Magazine*

p. 37

"... the tone, the coloring, the slate, the moss, the rockweed all astonish me; the place has an intellect, a countenance all its own."

Paraphrase of excerpt from Keats's letter to Tom, June 25–27, 1818

p. 40

"Naughty boy."

From Keats's poem "There was a Naughty Boy"

p. 49, 50

"a very pretty piece of paganism"

From Haydon's later account of the first meeting between Keats and Wordsworth

p. 49

"a leap headlong into the sea"

From Keats's letter to J. A. Hessey, October 8, 1818: "In Endymion I leaped headlong into the Sea."

p. 49

"a man of little knowledge and middling intellect"

Paraphrase of excerpt from Keats's letter to Haydon, March 8, 1819: "I am three and twenty, with little knowledge and middling intellect."

p. 51-55

Portions of the dialogue and events in the Immortal Dinner are modeled after Haydon's written account of the dinner.

p. 57

"I declared myself at your mercy. I confessed to you that I cannot live without you."

Paraphrase of excerpts from Keats's letters to Fanny Brawne, October 11, 1819 and May 20, 1820

p. 59

"… monstrous in her behavior, flying out in all directions, calling people such names—not from any innate vice but from a penchant she has for acting stylishly."

From Keats's letter to George and Georgina, December 1818

p. 66-67

"Negative Capability: allowing oneself to dwell in a state of uncertainties, mysteries, and doubts."

Paraphrase of excerpt from Keats's letter to George and Tom, December 1817: "… At once it struck me, what quality went to form a Man of Achievement, especially in Literature & which Shakespeare possessed so enormously—I mean Negative Capability, that is, when a man is capable of being in uncertainties, Mysteries, doubts, without any irritable reaching after fact & reason."

p. 75
"I am still dazzled by her. I am still at her mercy."

Paraphrase of excerpt from Keats's letter to Fanny Brawne, October 11, 1819: "I feel myself at your mercy. Write me ever so few lines … You dazzled me."

Author's Note:
Fanny Brawne has been the subject of considerable controversy over the decades. Was she a devoted lover? A heartless flirt? An affectionate but shallow young woman who had no idea of the extent of her fiancé's genius?

Some of the controversy, remarkably, centers on her use of a double negative in a letter that she penned to Charles Brown ten years after Keats's death, when Brown reached out to her while putting together a biography of his friend.

She wrote to Brown, "I should not now like the odium of being connected with one who was working up his way against poverty and every sort of abuse," and then added the key sentence, "I should be glad if you could disprove I was a very poor judge of character ten years ago and probably overrated every good quality he had."

The question is, does this letter catch her in the act of admitting that she "overrated" every good quality Keats had?

Or—because it's a double negative—is she asking Brown to assure her that she was not a poor judge of character, that she had not overrated his good qualities? In other words, "Tell me I wasn't wrong to love him."

This second interpretation seems more likely to me.

It might be worth remembering that at the time she wrote this letter, in 1831, Fanny was a member of the small circle that cherished the memory of Keats. It was at least ten or fifteen more years before Keats would find instant worldwide fame.

Also of note is this fact: though Fanny at first hid the engagement ring Keats gave her, after his death, without comment, she retrieved the ring and started to wear it. Telling no one its significance—not even Louis Lindo, the man she would marry fourteen years later in 1833—she wore the garnet ring upon her finger every day until her death.

p. 94
     "in a sort of temper indolent and supremely careless"

From Keats's letter to George and Georgina, February 19, 1819

Author's note: Keats claimed in the letter that he had a black eye from playing cricket, but it seems more likely to have resulted from the altercation over the treatment of the cat.

p. 95-97

Letter on the "vale of soul-making"

Keats's somewhat edited letter to George and Georgina, April 1819

p. 95

"Life must be undergone."

From Keats's letter to Benjamin Bailey, June 10, 1818, and Keats's "Ode to a Nightingale"

p. 97

"winding mossy ways"

From Keats's "Ode to a Nightingale"

p. 104

"I hope you love me for more than my 'beauty,' my dear boy." She strokes my hair.

"I do. But you can't blame me for being enraptured of your beauty." I bend forward for another kiss.

"I believe there was never another poet like you, John Keats. But I want you to know, I love you for who you are, and not because you are a poet."

"Thank God for that," I declare. "I have met women whom I really think would like to be married to a Poem and to be given away by a Novel."

From Keats's letter to Fanny Brawne, freely edited, July 8, 1819

p. 107

"I love you too much to venture to Hampstead. Knowing well that my life must be passed in fatigue and trouble, I have been endeavoring to wean myself from you, but I cannot cease to love you."

From Keats's letter to Fanny Brawne, somewhat edited, September 13, 1819

p. 116

"a dark and shapeless mass"

Paraphrase from Shelley's "The Waning Moon": "a white and shapeless mass"

p. 116

"… dissolving in a pool of water, the scale fades into …"

Paraphrase from Keats's "Ode to a Nightingale": "Fade far away, dissolve …"

p. 129

"I know the color," I tell him. "It is arterial blood; I cannot be deceived. That drop of blood is my death warrant—I must die."

This statement and some of the preceding dialogue are from Charles Brown's account of the evening.

p. 129–130

> This living hand, now warm and capable
> Of earnest grasping, would, if it were cold
> And in the icy silence of the tomb,
> So haunt thy days and chill thy dreaming nights
> That thou would wish thine own heart dry of blood
> So in my veins red life might stream again,
> And thou be conscience-calm'd—see here it is
> I hold it towards you.

Keats jotted this chilling verse in the margins of *The Cap and Bells,* a comedy for the stage that he worked on without success in late fall and early winter, 1819.

p. 132-133

Letter beginning "You could not step or move an eyelid but it would shoot to my heart"

From Keats's letter to Fanny Brawne, somewhat edited, May 1820

p. 142

"piled high like rich garners bursting with grain"

Paraphrase of Keats's "When I have fears that I may cease to be," lines 3 and 4

p. 155

"Severn—I—lift me up—I am dying—I shall die easy— don't be frightened—be firm, and thank God it has come!"

From Severn's account of the last days of John Keats.

p. 155

"borne aloft"

From Keats's "To Autumn"

p. 156

"capable of being in uncertainties"

From Keats's letter to George and Thomas, December 21, 1817

p. 156

"He is unsure if he wakes or sleeps."

Paraphrase of excerpt from Keats's "Ode to a Nightingale"

CPSIA information can be obtained
at www.ICGtesting.com
Printed in the USA
LVHW031934021221
705102LV00004B/155